Waiting for a Sign

Esty Schachter

ISBN: 0692286985
ISBN 13: 9780692286982
Library of Congress Control Number: 2014915790
Lewis Court Press, Ithaca, NY

Waiting for a Sign

Also by Esty Schachter

Anya's Echoes

For Lisa

If this book were a movie, it would be bilingual, in American Sign Language and spoken English. American Sign Language is a rich, visual language, with its own complex grammar. Since it is not possible to show the beauty and dimension of sign language in written text, I have translated into English the passages expressed in ASL by Ian and other characters, and those translations appear in this book as italicized text.

1

I do it all the time, and I don't know why.

I creep up behind my brother's back, sneer something like "Mom likes me better" or "You are so annoying," and then wait to see if he'll turn around. He won't, not unless he feels the vibration of my steps through the floor, or somehow sees me out of the corner of his eye.

This time, Ian didn't move. He sat in his chair, his head bent over his desk.

I crept in closer as he concentrated on replacing the battery in his watch. Inch by inch, I moved in until I was practically breathing down his neck. Unfortunately, I must have actually breathed on him, because Ian quickly turned around and grabbed my arm.

"*What do you want?*" he signed angrily. I shoved him and ran to my room, slamming the door in his face.

Now, there's a part of me that knows that a girl who's turning fifteen is way too old to be playing cat-and-mouse with her eighteen-year-old brother. But baiting Ian started way back, six long years back, when he went away to school, and eventually it became a habit. During the week, Ian lives at the Hawthorne School for the Deaf, two hours away. I only see him on weekends.

I pressed my ear against the door, listening for any sounds of movement on the other side. Ian likes to wait me out and then pounce on me once I think the coast is clear. But I'm not falling for that one anymore. He may not have been around to notice, but I'm smarter than I used to be.

Once he started going to Hawthorne, Ian spent his weekends moping around the house, missing his new friends. When he got bored enough, he started looking for ways to amuse himself. He threw balls of rolled-up tape at me while I did my homework. He poked me under the dinner table and then when I yelled, looked innocently at our parents. He'd mess around with my violin and say he was trying to appreciate music.

Since he hit high school, though, he's given up on me altogether. And I've pretty much given up on him, too.

The door bell rang, meaning my best friend Lisa was outside, waiting for me to let her in. I didn't move, and she rang again. I knew she was tapping her foot, wondering where in the world I could be.

I swung the bedroom door open, fast. So fast, I stubbed my big toe against it. I couldn't wait to catch Ian waiting to catch me. But he wasn't there. The long hallway was empty. My toe hurt like crazy, and Ian was gone.

I hobbled down the stairs and opened the front door. Lisa walked in, dragging a suitcase, backpack, and sleeping bag behind her.

"What took you so long, Shelly?" she asked.

I grabbed the sleeping bag and ignored the question. "Are you moving in?" I asked incredulously.

She rolled her eyes and laughed. "I never know when I might need something."

"For one night?"

"Hey, I've got extra jeans and two shirts, a sweater if I'm cold, shorts if I get hot, pajamas, toothbrush, two books we have to read for English, three magazines and my journal. Are you limping?"

I was too embarrassed to tell her the whole story, so I just shrugged it off. "Stubbed my toe."

We dragged her stuff up the stairs, down the hall and into my room. "I really think you've run away from home," I said. "You could stay in Ian's room if he wasn't here."

"He's back already? Cool." Lisa said cheerfully.

"Yeah. He's back." I said in the dullest, dreariest voice I could muster.

Lisa didn't seem to notice. "That's great. He isn't going to miss dinner."

I rolled my eyes. "Yeah, really great. Try getting me on the computer when he's using the videophone. Try getting me a ride when he's got the car. Forget it. I barely exist on the weekends with him around, and soon it could be all the time."

All anyone could talk about for the last few months was the news that the Hawthorne School for the Deaf might close. State decision. Budget cuts. Ian could lose his school, and I would get him back, full-time, for good. Nightmare? Yeah.

We plunked ourselves down on the floor of my room. I grabbed the tennis magazine sticking out of Lisa's bag and looked through it.

"Is there a story on Marcus Moore in here?" I asked.

Lisa didn't answer. She leaned back on her elbows, glancing out the door towards Ian's room.

"Hello! Earth to Lisa!" I whacked her on the head with the magazine.

"Ow!" Lisa rubbed her head. "What?"

I danced the magazine in front of my face. "Marcus Moore? Yes? No?" He currently held the title of our favorite tennis player, and Lisa's fiancé, at least in her highly imaginative mind.

Lisa suddenly remembered she was supposed to be talking to me. She shook her head. "Nope. But I got it anyway. There's an article on Wimbledon." Lisa moved closer and we flipped through pages of professional tennis players together, until she suddenly sat back and looked at me. "I keep meaning to talk to you about your birthday. What are we going to do?" she asked.

I shrugged. "Nothing much. My parents claimed Friday night for our family birthday dinner, and you're at that tennis banquet Saturday night."

I twirled my hair into a bun and then let it fall apart again. I didn't want to tell Lisa the real reason I hadn't planned a party. Since word came out that Hawthorne might close, our house had taken on the atmosphere of a war zone. Friday night always meant some kind of fight between Ian and my parents. It was as if he suddenly couldn't stand a single thing we said or did. Last week Mom made the mistake of asking how his Biology test went. The week before, Dad dared to say he ought to get his laundry done. Really controversial stuff.

Lisa turned and tossed the magazine onto my bed. "How about I sleep over again next Friday night? Ask your parents if I can crash your family dinner."

I spun a lock of hair around my finger and didn't say anything.

She smiled craftily. "I happen to know your birthday is going to be a very good day."

"Oh, yeah?" I asked warily.

"Yup," she nodded. "Absolutely. No doubt about it." And she started to sing.

That's Lisa for you. One minute you're sitting around, having a conversation, and the next, she serenades you with whatever song pops into her head. This time it was "Happy Birthday," of course, but the full opera version, no holding back. After her song, she collapsed on the bed, laughing. And I was laughing too. Lisa's singing is my own personal soundtrack. Someday she'll probably send me tickets to her opening night on Broadway.

If you haven't figured it out yet, I save my singing for the shower.

"Please?" she asked, her hands clasped under her chin. "Will you ask your parents?"

Lisa knows how to get at that little part of me that wants to say yes when I'm about to say no. This is how she convinced me to go skiing for the first time. And got me to read a poem I'd written, out loud, to my English class.

"Okay, okay, I'll ask them," I said. Who was I kidding? Lisa wasn't about to let my birthday slip by unnoticed. Not a chance.

"Girls! Dinner!" My mom yelled up the stairs. "Shelly, get your brother."

We got up, and my stomach hurt from laughing so much. Lisa went to the bathroom. Ian's door was closed, so I pounded on it a couple of times. Nothing happened. I knocked again, and when Ian didn't come to the door, I opened it and stuck my head inside. Ian had his back to me, naked. He turned slightly and startled at the sight of me, then grabbed a towel and held it in front of him.

"What are you doing in here?" he asked angrily, signing with his one free hand. *"Go away!"*

I shut the door quickly, then realized I hadn't mentioned dinner. I hit my head softly against the wall.

Lisa came out of the bathroom and came up behind me. "What's up? Why are you doing that?"

Just then, Ian opened the door. *"Am I allowed to get dressed in private? Is that allowed here?"* he asked.

"Mom told me to call you for dinner. I didn't..." But Ian was already down the stairs.

"What happened?" Lisa whispered.

I shook my head. "You don't want to know."

We went downstairs and sat at the table. The room smelled of tomato sauce and sautéed onions. My mother served eggplant parmesan to each of us while my father poured glasses of water. They were both still dressed in their work clothes, a sure sign that they were rushed and stressed. My mother's nametag was pinned to her dinosaur shirt. She's a nurse in a pediatrician's office. My father still had on the usual shirt and tie combination he wears for his job at the auto dealership downtown. My father hates ties.

Ian scowled at me. I mouthed, "I didn't know" to him across the table. He shook me off. I looked down at my plate. I got it. It didn't matter that I hadn't really seen anything. It's not like I would want him walking in on me either.

My parents sat down and my mother sighed softly. "I am exhausted," she said. "I didn't sleep well last night. Did you hear that wind?" she asked my father.

They started talking about the weather, while I continued to fend off nasty glares from across the table. My mother turned to Lisa and asked about her tennis tournament schedule. Lisa does it all: she has a beautiful voice and sings in three different choruses, gets great grades in school, and is a star on the tennis team. I watch and wonder how.

Lisa told them about how the coach was having the team practice late some nights, and how hard it was to get all her work done. "The new coach is great though, he really knows his stuff. I'm learning a lot."

"I played in high school," my mom said, as she served herself some salad. "I loved the matches but I hated the travel."

"I don't really mind it," Lisa said. "I listen to music most of the time. And it's nice to hang out with the other girls."

I looked over at Ian. Now he was glaring at my parents as they talked to Lisa. He had barely eaten any of his eggplant, and was just staring at them, hard. A moment later he got up and walked out of the room.

"Where's Ian going?" Mom asked.

"Probably the bathroom," Dad said, chewing on a piece of bread.

When Ian came back, he was holding a book. *The Catcher in the Rye*. He sat down at the table, opened it, and started reading and eating his dinner.

"Ian!" my mother said, and waved her hand to get his attention. Ian kept reading.

"Ian." Dad reached over and put his hand on Ian's shoulder. "What are you doing?" he asked, speaking and signing. "Put the book down."

Ian leaned back in his chair. *"Stop reading? Why? No one is talking to me. You're not signing. I have no idea what you're talking about. I have to read this book for school, so I'm going to read it now."*

He flipped a page, scooping food into his mouth as he read. My parents sat, frozen. Lisa and I looked at each other, wondering what would happen next. Dad glanced at my mother, then he reached over, took the book out of Ian's hands, and dropped it on the floor. He looked at Ian.

"We were talking about Lisa's tennis practice." He signed and spoke slowly, then hesitated. "If you've got a problem, say something. But leave the attitude somewhere else."

My dad picked up his fork and started eating again. We all did. It was something to do. I looked over at Ian. His expression was distant and cold, not playful like it used to be. In the old days, he would tell us story after story from school, practically acting each one out at the table. He could be three characters at the same time by simply shifting his body in his chair, or changing his facial expression. I loved watching him. My parents and I always asked for more. When had he stopped telling stories?

We ate silently for more than five minutes. Five minutes feels like an hour in the war zone. I couldn't think of anything to say, and it was clear I wasn't the only one.

"Shel," my mother began, signing my name sign as she said it aloud, "What was the name of that shampoo you wanted from the store?"

Saved by shampoo! "I don't know," I said and signed. "I used it at Catherine's house and it smelled great. It comes in a bright green bottle."

"I'm going to need more information than that," Mom said. "You can come with me tomorrow."

"Sure," I said. I used a bit of garlic bread to wipe the tomato sauce off my plate, then popped it into my mouth, eyeing Ian the whole time.

Ian put down his knife and fork. *"May I be excused?"* he asked, signing stiffly.

Dad nodded his head. Ian got up and left the table, and a moment later we heard his door slam. My parents looked at each other.

"It's going to be a long road," Dad said.

"I meant to tell you," Mom began, "the social worker from school called me at work. She says he's really struggling with all the talk about Hawthorne closing. He's hardly done any of his work, and he got into a fight last week. She says it's understandable, but..."

"What kind of fight?"

"Just some shoving. Nothing major. But definitely out of the ordinary for him at school."

Dad sighed. "We had to expect it. I just don't want it to get out of hand." He moved his salad around his plate with his fork.

Lisa and I looked at each other. She wrinkled her nose at me. That was my cue.

"Can we be excused too?" I asked.

"See you later," Dad said.

We put our dishes in the sink and escaped to my room.

"That was intense," Lisa said.

"No kidding. Glad you could be here for our little family soap opera." I realized I was biting my thumbnail.

Lisa shrugged. "I feel really bad for Ian. I'd hate it if someone told me I might have to change schools right before my senior year. And that's without the deaf part."

"Yeah, I know." Lisa was right, of course. And I did feel bad for Ian. It wasn't fair at all. I could see all of Ian's arguments in my head. How could he switch to a new school? What about his friends? At the school near home, he would need an interpreter in every class. What if the interpreter was late, or sick? No one at the high school in our neighborhood knew how to sign. No one other than me, that is.

I don't want to be alone.

I did understand. What I didn't say to Lisa, though, was that he wasn't the only one who was dealing with the problem. He was making all of us deal with it too, whether we wanted to or not.

2

I woke up on my birthday with the worst case of bed-head imaginable.

I pulled a brush through my dark blonde hair, splashed water on my bangs, and finally gave up, dunking my whole head under the shower.

On days when I get out of bed fifteen minutes before I'm supposed to leave for school, I absolutely do not have time for last-minute hair emergencies. I left the house with my hair dripping down my back and a muffin in my hand. It took me just under four minutes to run all six blocks to school.

I slipped into my seat just as the late bell went off. My homeroom teacher, Mr. Polin, nodded at me. I can never tell if the nod means, "You made it" or "That's correct, tardy again." He's a social studies teacher, very proper, and his small gestures mean everything, if you understand them. When he's teaching, a swipe of his finger across his forehead means "Well done," but a tap of that same finger on his chin means, "You haven't got a clue." I did a double-take as I realized Mr. Polin was walking towards me. He stepped up to my desk, holding a package wrapped in comic strip paper.

"Happy Birthday, Miss Marks. I hope it's a good one."
He placed the package in front of me, then turned on his
heel and walked back to his desk. I suddenly became the
center of all homeroom attention as I unwrapped the package to reveal a giant chocolate bar. A note on top read,
"From L. and C., because a birthday girl you be!"

I looked over at Lisa and Catherine, snickering in the
corner. Our last names all begin with the letter "M", Marks,
Mead, Meyer, so we get to have homeroom together. Lisa
waved. I stuck my tongue out at her. My homeroom broke
out in an off-key rendition of "Happy Birthday," and to
make them stop, I snapped off a piece of chocolate and
passed the rest around.

Lisa, Catherine, and Macie – our fourth Musketeer –
were just getting started. At the beginning of every class
for the rest of the day, each teacher presented me with a
wrapped piece of candy, and a wish for a happy birthday.
By the end of the day, I was both a news item and suffering
from serious sugar shock. A person can always depend on
her true friends to mortify her on her birthday.

Lisa ran up to my locker after school. "You are so bad,"
I said, handing her a peanut butter cup.

"That's right, I am." She beamed. "Wasn't Mr. Polin hysterical? 'Happy Birthday, Miss Marks,'" she mimicked in a
robot voice.

"I had no idea what was going on. No idea." I looked at
my hair in my locker mirror. Not bad for dunk-and-run hair.

"Did Mr. You-Know-Who say anything?" she asked,
leaning over and letting her long, brown hair sweep the
floor. She brushed it, starting at the back of her head and
working downwards.

Mr. You-Know-Who is a very cute, very tall guy with
beautiful, stop-you-in-your-tracks eyes. He wears white or

black turtlenecks that look great against his dark skin, and he doesn't talk much. At least, not to us. He'd just started going to our New Jersey high school, moving all the way from California. We liked to think he was a quiet, creative type, a budding journalist or photographer, but mostly, we liked to look at him.

Lisa and I both had a thing for him. Once, when we were walking home from school, she said something about him being the most gorgeous guy in our grade, and I said something about his unbelievable eyes, and the next thing we knew, we were standing in the middle of the street revealing how we each felt about him. That is, until a pick-up rushed by and the driver shouted, "Get out of the road!" which we promptly did. Strange as it may seem, it can be a lot of fun sharing a crush with your best friend.

"So?" she asked again, brushing the ends.

I didn't answer. If I was going to divulge anything, I wanted her full attention. Lisa lifted her head quickly, and her mane of hair flew behind her. "I can't hear you...!" she taunted.

"Yeah, yeah, he said happy birthday," I said shyly.

"Yes!" Lisa shouted, pumping her fist. "Smile or no smile?"

I had to think about that. "I can't remember. But he kind of leaned in, sort of."

"Very nice."

Catherine and Macie arrived at my locker, smiling devilishly. Macie bent down and pulled her long socks up over her skinny knees. Macie doesn't like her knees. She says they're boney and too thin, so wearing a skirt means she also wears extra-long socks to cover them with. But since they were always slipping down, Macie ended up looking like a little kid wearing clothes three sizes too big.

Catherine, on the other hand, is always dressed as if she'd just walked out of a fashion catalog. Matching everything. Her closets and drawers are color-coded. She even has some kind of filing system going on in her locker. That girl is organized.

"Is she ready?" Macie asked.

"What are you guys talking about?" I asked, even though I figured I was about to find out.

Lisa took a scarf out of her backpack. "Ready, team?" she asked, in her best secret agent voice. The next thing I knew, Lisa covered my eyes with the scarf and tied it behind my head.

"Hello? What are you guys doing?"

"You are being kidnapped," Lisa said. "It's for your own good. We are saving you from the unfortunate fate of not doing anything to celebrate your birthday."

I laughed. "Very funny. Okay, take the blindfold off."

"No." And with that, I was led down the hall, Lisa on one side, Macie on the other. I heard my locker slam behind me. "Where exactly are you taking me?" I asked.

"Obviously, a surprise," Catherine said, giggling. Her clogs clip-clopped past me.

They led me through the door, letting me know when I needed to step down. As we began walking, I heard Macie laughing quietly, along with the soft bump of the backpacks against our backs. I picked out a siren in the distance. Lisa and Macie had not worked on coordinating their movements, so I stumbled along and tried to keep up as one led me from the right and the other from the left. Every so often they would suddenly move to one side or the other, apparently guiding me around puddles and dog poop.

"How far are you going to make me do this? It is my birthday, you know."

"Just a few more miles," Lisa teased.

I moaned. Cars whizzed past us on the road. I considered the fact that there were too many cars for the quiet road that led to my house. "You're not making me walk like this all the way to Nassau Street, are you?" More laughter and giggles. "No way! This is the kind of thing you do when someone turns ten, not fifteen," I complained.

"If only you'd made your own plans," Macie said.

"What's this all about?" It was a man's voice. Great, I thought, spectators.

"It's her birthday!" Catherine announced.

"Happy birthday, young lady!" he shouted as we walked past.

"Shoot, we should have made a sign that said "Honk for the birthday girl," Lisa said, faking disappointment. "Oh well, next year."

"There is no way I'm letting any of you near me next year!" I shouted.

"Don't worry," Lisa said, squeezing my arm, "we're almost there."

I could tell we were on Nassau by the sounds and smells that hovered around each shop. I could feel steam on my face as we passed the laundry, and the smell of cinnamon, dough and sugar that hung in the air around the bakery.

I love that bakery. When I was a kid, there was nothing better than standing in front of the glass case full of dozens of different cookies. "Pick any one you want," my grandmother would say in her Russian accent. Ian and I would stand there as long as she'd let us, choosing between half-moons, rugelach, chocolate chip, and cinnamon-swirled pastries. Then she'd take us by the hand and we'd walk down Nassau, just like I was doing now. I'd listen for the birds chirping inside the pet store, and sometimes we'd step inside to watch hamsters run on metal wheels in their cages. We'd hold our noses in the butcher shop, hovering near the door.

The last stop on our weekly shopping trip was Muddy's, the ice cream store. Mom and Dad let Grandma buy a pint a week to send home with us. Ian and I negotiated the flavor. We stood by the counter, fingerspelling *mint chocolate chip*, *vanilla fudge*, and *cherry jubilee* back and forth until we agreed. Once I tried to trick him to get my own way. We couldn't settle on what to buy, and I pretended to give in, plotting to simply order the flavor I wanted when the man at the counter asked. I was the interpreter, always. When I spoke, Ian, watching me closely, saw the lie on my lips. He was angry, but worse, I saw that I had betrayed him. I never did anything like that again.

Macie tripped on the sidewalk and almost pulled me down with her. The smell of hot fudge was overpowering, and I knew we'd arrived at the ice cream shop. That's where we had to be going – one more stop in Lisa, Catherine and Macie's plan to kill me with sugar.

"Are we there yet?" I asked.

"Nope," Lisa said. "You sure are testy for a birthday girl."

We kept walking. Past the bank, the convenience store, the movie house. The movies! The smell of buttered popcorn wafted around us. What could they be taking me to see?

We kept walking.

At the traffic light at the end of the block, Lisa and Macie led me left, and we walked a bit more until they finally stopped. "Here we are!" Catherine said, pulling off the scarf.

I stared up at the bowling alley. "You're joking, right?"

"No, no, no. We're all going bowling. This is going to be great," Lisa said, grabbing my arm.

"You're supposed to be nice to someone on their birthday. Didn't you know that?"

Macie took hold of my other arm and together they pulled me inside. Before I knew it, I was wearing an ugly pair of red and white bowling shoes, well worn-in by countless other size six bowlers.

"They pinch," I said, pouting.

"You're such a cute complainer," Macie said, pinching my cheeks like my grandmother used to.

"Let's go, ladies." Lisa called, and we joined her at lanes 13 and 14. I sat down in the blue plastic chair next to her. "Macie and Catherine against me and Shelly Sunshine, okay?"

I poked her in the ribs. "Ow!" she faked, and tickled me back.

Lisa stood up and carefully selected an appropriately weighted ball that just happened to be shocking pink. She walked slowly up to the lane, brought her arm back, and propelled it forward. The ball slid down the lane while Lisa moved her arms and hips back and forth, encouraging her pink ball on its journey. The three of us fell over in hysterics at Lisa's bowling dance, but she knocked down eight pins. Not too bad!

We bowled without any of Lisa's fancy moves to dismal results. As Macie's ball rolled into the gutter for the seventh time, she threw up her hands and shouted, "Oh, forget it!" Her ball returned, spat up by the automatic machine to our left, and Macie practically threw it down the lane, accompanied by nothing less than a hula dance. She swayed her hips in slow circles, socks bunched way down at her ankles. She moved her arms like ocean waves. I laughed so hard I almost choked on the potato chip in my mouth.

But the competition had begun. Each turn meant a new dance move. Catherine is almost as shy as I am when it comes to moving one's body to music. We tend to keep each other company at school dances, sipping soda and gossiping. Still, with Lisa shouting encouragement from her blue chair, I pretended to be a ballerina as I tossed the ball down the lane. Catherine showed us some robot moves, which left us hunched over.

Our bowling scores didn't improve, but after an hour my ribs hurt from laughing so much. By the end of two games, Lisa had everyone in the bowling alley cheering us on. Granted, there were only five other people in the place at four-thirty on a Friday afternoon, but they were with us all the way.

We stumbled out of the bowling alley a short while later. There was only one way to describe how I felt. I was happy, pure and simple. I hugged each of the girls tightly, and then Lisa and I made our way home.

"Great day," I said.

Lisa beamed. "I knew it would be."

We walked into my house, collapsing on the couch. I closed my eyes, and thought back on the silliness of the day. I heard my parents in the kitchen.

"How could he forget?" my mother said. That got me listening.

"I don't know. Maybe he didn't forget. All I know is, Ian called from Mario's house to say he was staying there for the weekend and I gave him hell. I told him to get himself home tomorrow."

"How's he going to do that? Mario lives out in Bellingham."

"I don't know. I don't care. Maybe he'll ask Mario's parents. He'll probably catch a bus." I didn't hear anything for a minute. I realized I was holding my breath. "I don't think he forgot," my dad continued, "but there's no reason he should take this out on her."

"At least Lisa's here," Mom said. "Shelly deserves to have a good birthday."

I heard the clank of plates knocking against each other as my parents emptied the dishwasher and put the dishes away. "Did you hear that?" I asked Lisa.

"What?"

"My brother is skipping my birthday dinner," I said flatly. Lisa sat up. "He probably just forgot. He would never do something like that on purpose."

"How do you know?" I said. I put the couch pillow over my face, muffling my words. "He doesn't care."

Lisa put her hand on my knee. "We'll have a great time, anyway." She poked the pillow. "Tell your parents you want to go out for sushi."

I smiled under the pillow. Lisa always knew how to make a bad situation better. She would point out the positive comments teachers wrote on my essays when I obsessed about the corrections. She was happy if it was sunny outside, and just as happy when it rained. It could have been annoying if it wasn't so honest. It was simply who she was. I tossed the pillow on the floor and sat up. "That's for me, right? You wouldn't want to go out for sushi. You'll only do it if you have to," I teased.

"If I have to," she said solemnly.

My parents agreed. The restaurant was decorated with thousands of paper cranes, strung on wire and hanging from the ceiling. The flock created an ocean of color. Lisa and I stuffed ourselves with slippery orange salmon, reddish-pink tuna, and half a dozen types of fish whose names we didn't know. We sipped green tea out of small ceramic cups, and ordered lychee fruit and ice cream for dessert.

"I love all those birds," I said quietly. I took a breath and blew on the ones hanging above our table, and they moved gently in the wind. When the waitress came with our check, Lisa said she had a question for her.

"Can you teach me how to make an origami crane?" she asked.

"Sure," the waitress said and returned a few moments later with a square sheet of blue paper. She leaned over the table next to Lisa's chair and began to fold the paper this way and that, until, at last, she held a crane in her palm and handed it to Lisa. Lisa placed it in front of me.

"Happy Birthday, Shel," she whispered.

That night, I pulled my blankets up to my neck and rolled over onto my side. The crane rested on my night table. I looked down at Lisa, nestled into her sleeping bag like it was a cocoon. We could talk like this all night, lights out, flashlight on, and a whole week of school to pick over. Mr. You-Know-Who alone was good for hours worth of conversation. We'd already covered quite a bit of ground on him, as well as reviewing all the details of my birthday. I yawned and glanced over at the clock glowing 3:00 in the dark.

Lisa looked up at the ceiling. "Shel?"

"Yeah?"

"I've got to ask you something." She sounded uncertain, and I wasn't used to hearing that in her voice.

"What?"

"You'll always tell me the truth, right?"

"Of course. Lisa, what's the matter?"

She turned over on her side. "Am I sometimes too much? You know, with singing and stuff like that. Is it just too much sometimes?"

"I have no idea what you're talking about," I said, and then I paused. "Did someone say something to you?"

Lisa exhaled. "Yeah. Seneca Hale. She said she longed for the day I would just shut my mouth." Lisa mimicked Seneca's high-pitched voice. "She said I always have something to say about everything, and no one else has a chance..." Lisa's voice withered at the end.

"Look, there are always going to be people who are jealous of you. You beat Seneca out for a solo in the choir performance. She's mad at you. That was a stupid thing for her to say." Lisa and I looked at each other, our heads resting on our pillows. "It's not true."

"You sure?" she asked again, so that I knew how much Seneca had gotten to her.

"Very sure. Very, very sure. I want you to be exactly the way you are. If I wasn't such a mouse, I'd go yell at Seneca for you."

Lisa laughed at the idea. She reached over and squeezed my arm. "Thanks, Shel. Really. You're such a great friend."

After that, we talked some more about Macie's new dog and Catherine's new crush. Our voices got slower and quieter. Lisa fell asleep in the middle of a sentence.

3

On Sunday morning, Lisa called and asked me to meet her at the park to play tennis. My parents were already gone, off to do errands at the mall. After I dragged my bike out of the garage, I saw that the front tire was completely flat. Ian's bike was leaning against the wall, showing off its healthy air-filled tires.

I walked back through the house and poked my head into his room. Ian was lying on his bed, throwing a basketball at the wall. He'd gotten back from Mario's late on Saturday. He'd dropped a card on my bed and signed *Happy Birthday* before walking out of the room again.

"I need to borrow your bike. I've got a flat," I said and signed.

"*What?*"

The ball hit the wall, once, twice. Ian was barely looking at me.

"The tire on my bike's flat. I need to borrow your bike."

"*What?*"

Ian shot the ball against the wall, hard.

"Stop doing that!" I shouted as I signed.

"*Stop talking when you sign! I can't understand you!*" Ian signed roughly.

I stepped back. My stomach felt as if he he'd hit me. His face was red and clenched like a fist. I had never seen him so angry. I turned and ran to my room, but this time he caught me before I could slam the door in his face.

"I'm sorry," he signed.

"Go away!" I turned away from him. I didn't want him to see me crying.

He took hold of my shoulders and tried to turn me towards him. I shook him off and ran to the other end of the room, where I leaned against my chest of drawers and glared at his reflection in the mirror.

"Get out!"

He didn't move.

"Do you understand this sign?" I asked, then held up my middle finger.

It stuck out in the air, ugly and strange. I had never, ever cursed like that before, not out of my mouth or on my hands, and I think Ian knew it. I expected him to respond in kind, to curse me out and then leave. But I was wrong.

Ian's face in the mirror looked different now; it was softer, and the hateful look was gone. He looked sad and tired.

"I'm sorry. I don't know why I got so angry. I didn't mean to hurt your feelings."

I turned around so I could see him.

"I <u>need</u> to talk." I told him, speaking and signing at the same time. "I talk!"

"I know, but... Ian moved back, and went to my bed and sat down. *"But when you talk, sometimes you forget to sign."*

"What are you talking about?"

"Like before, I saw you signing 'bike' and 'borrow' and 'flat,' but I had to guess the other words from looking at your mouth." Ian

sighed. *"I knew what you were trying to tell me, but it made me mad. It always makes me mad. It happens all the time. You do it; Mom and Dad do it."* Ian ran his hands through his hair. He looked me in the eye. *"I want to know what you're saying. I want to know all of what you tell me."*

"But I don't sign well enough anymore."

"That's ridiculous. You sign fine. Your signing is great. Like always. Remember when we were little, and you were the only one who could understand me? Remember when you had to tell everyone what I wanted to say?"

I nodded. When we were younger, before Mom and Dad agreed to let Ian go to Hawthorne, we went to the same school. He had an interpreter in class, but when it came to the playground or with friends at home, I was his interpreter. Sometimes even with Mom and Dad. It seemed easier for me to learn to sign, as if my fingers were elastic, and it became like our secret language. I liked that. I liked being the only one who really understood him. I sat down on the bed across from Ian.

"I guess...." I started to speak and sign and stopped. *"Maybe I didn't realize how much it mattered. Maybe... I wasn't sure you cared."*

Ian nodded. *"I do, and it makes sense, not just for me, but for you, also. Just one language, not two."*

"Okay," I signed. American Sign Language and English. One language at a time, not two. English and ASL were completely different, I knew that. They had two different grammars, two whole different ways of communicating. By trying to use them at the same time, Ian understood me less, not more.

We sat there on my bed, facing each other. It had been a long time since Ian and I had talked about anything, especially something so important. There was something else, something that had been bothering me for a long time, and before I could stop myself, the signs began to slip off my fingers.

"You know," I started, *"when we were little you played with me all the time, and then you started going to Hawthorne, and got all new friends, and you stopped. You didn't do anything with me anymore. I felt like you... traded me in for something better.* I took a deep breath. *I really missed you."*

Ian stared at me, his eyes wide, and suddenly I wished I hadn't said anything. His cheeks turned red again, but this time he was biting his lip, the way he does when he's upset. He shook his head.

"Trade you? You're my sister, I would never..." Ian stopped, and took a breath. He looked away, and I could feel my heart bouncing like a tennis ball inside my chest.

Ian looked back at me. *"It was just that it was the first time I felt so... free. I didn't have to think about communicating, I just did. I could pick my friends. I could laugh and argue and tell jokes and cheat on tests... Here, it's like I'm in a fishbowl. Mom and Dad talk and sometimes forget to sign, and I sit and watch everyone. I don't want to watch. I want to be part of everything."*

"So don't walk away from us." I said, looking Ian in the eye. *"Don't pretend you don't care about my birthday."*

Ian put his hand on my shoulder. *"I'm sorry, really."* Ian stared at me, his head tilted to the side. *"I miss you too."* He reached over and hugged me tightly. When he leaned back, he was smiling.

"Enough," he signed. *"Enough talking.... about... serious stuff..."* He fell back on the bed, hands around his throat, tongue hanging out, as if he had been poisoned. He looked at me, to see if it would make me laugh now, the same way it did when we were younger. It still worked.

Ian smiled. *"What are you doing now?"*

I smacked the side of my head with my palm. *"Lisa's waiting for me at the park! I forgot all about her!"*

I told Ian about my tire, and asked if I could borrow his bike.

"Sure," he answered, and got up to walk to the door. He stopped and looked at me. *"Can I come with you?"*

"Okay, but... why?"

Ian shrugged. *"Why not?"*

Ian and I walked to the garage, and he grabbed his bike. We searched for the pump, turning over old tires, lawn chairs and a plastic sled until we found it, tucked behind a stack of newspapers. I knelt and attached the end of the pump to the flat tire of my bike as Ian pushed air into it. Within minutes my tire ballooned back to normal. He squeezed it to make sure, and then paused.

"If you wanted to hang out with me, why did you annoy me all the time?" he asked, smirking.

"Me annoy you?" If hands could spit out words, I was spitting. *"Are you kidding?"*

"Yeah, I bothered you a little. You annoyed me all the time."

"That is so not true!"

Ian was beaming. He shrugged his shoulders. Then he hopped on his bike and rode off, an old trick. Get her mad, and then get a head start. I jumped on my bike and chased after him.

Ian and I raced each other to the park. As we got closer, I could see Lisa leaning on the metal fence which ringed the tennis court, arms crossed. As soon as she saw Ian though, her arms flew up and she waved. He got there first, screeching to a stop, dirt and pebbles flying into the air. Lisa smiled at him and signed hello. She smiled a fake smile at me and said, "What happened to you? I've been waiting for half an hour."

"Sorry," I said, "something came up." I was speaking and signing again. I looked down at my hands, not sure what to do.

Ian saw my awkwardness, and put his hand on my shoulder. *"It's okay."* He smiled confidently, grabbing a tennis racket out of the bike basket. *"I'm playing. Who wants to lose first?"*

Ian ran onto the court, and Lisa followed. I sat down cross-legged and leaned against the fence. I didn't care if I'd been left behind to be a spectator. It felt good. It felt even better to watch Lisa, star of the tennis team, beat Ian point after point. He took it well, holding onto his heart as if he was dying of embarrassment, and staring, shocked, after her really good shots. Lisa won. They both walked off the court, sweating and laughing.

"Great game," Ian said, and I interpreted for Lisa.

"I understood him," Lisa said to me, and turned to Ian. "You, too," she said as she signed the words. "You play very well." There were long pauses between signs, but Ian understood her.

"Where did you learn sign language?" Ian asked, signing slowly and clearly.

"Yeah, where did you learn sign language?" I asked incredulously.

Lisa shrugged. "I got a video from the library," she said. She fingerspelled video. I have to admit, I was impressed. Lisa wanted to look casual, but it was pretty obvious she'd been working on this signing thing for a while.

"Cool." Ian nodded, and then wiped away sweat that had dripped off his forehead and into his eyes. He smiled, his blue eyes shining. *"I need a shower. I'll see you guys later."*

Lisa waved as Ian hopped on his bike and headed towards home. He turned around and waved back.

"Wow," Lisa breathed.

"Wow, what?"

"Your brother, stupid. He's so cute." Lisa collapsed on the ground, lying back on the grass. "And he gave me a work-out."

"Give me a break." I sat down next to Lisa. "You've been playing too much tennis. It's doing weird stuff to your head."

"You just haven't noticed because he's your brother. He's got those amazing blue eyes and I like how his hair gets curly when it's long."

I made a grossed-out face, but in fact, I was fascinated. "You started learning sign language so you could talk to my brother?"

"No, it's just some cosmic coincidence," she said. "Of course I got the video so I could figure out how to talk to him! He's the only Deaf person I know."

I used my nail to pick at a scab on my knee. "Why didn't you just ask me?" I asked.

Lisa shrugged. "I don't know. I never thought of asking you. I saw the video in the library, and I took it out. I've had it for two months; I'm the queen of renewals."

I ripped up some grass and tossed it at Lisa's feet. "Are you giving up on Mr. You-Know-Who?"

"No way! I'm just multi-tasking. I can handle more than one crush at a time." Lisa took a swig of water, and then dumped the rest of the bottle on her head, laughing as she did.

It's hard to explain, but it bothered me a lot that Lisa started learning sign language but hadn't told me about it. She talked to me about most of the things she did, so to leave this out was bigger than it seemed. Lisa hadn't known us in the old days, in the "Team Ian and Shelly" days. She had met me later, in middle school, in my I-don't-talk-about-my-brother period. She hadn't told me because it never occurred to her to say anything. And that was my fault.

Sometimes you can feel change happening just as it happens, the first moment, like a cool rain that starts suddenly on a warm day. I liked the feel of the drizzle on my face; I didn't expect it would turn into a storm.

4

For the next few weeks, Lisa became a regular at our house. I no longer cared about what she might happen to see, because the fact was, things were better. The war zone had cooled down, and now there were only occasional battles, rather than all-out conflict. Ian spent less time hiding away in his room or off by himself with his skateboard. Instead, he rushed me to finish my homework so that we might play some tennis, or shoot baskets in the hoop outside. Sometimes we rented movies. I looked forward to Ian coming home on weekends, and that felt good.

One Saturday evening we both had work to do, so he came into my room with his backpack and stack of books and we spread our papers and notebooks on the floor. He worked on an essay about civil rights and segregation while I scribbled complicated calculations into a notebook. When I needed a break, I asked Ian about his friends at school, and what his teachers were like. Ian's descriptions of one teacher, Mrs. Culpepper, with her overdone make-up and flashy clothes, had me rolling on the floor. Ian laughed until tears came to his eyes.

"She's a good teacher, though. She just always looks like the minute school is over, she leaves us to go dancing," he said, wiping his eyes. *"Maybe she does."*

I described Mr. Polin, emphasizing his crisp, robot walk.

"Oh yeah, Lisa told me about him."

Lisa told him about Mr. Polin? I stared at my notebook for a moment. So Lisa had told him about Mr. Polin. What was so weird about that?

Ian leaned on his elbow, pulling *To Kill a Mockingbird* out of his backpack. Lisa had wanted me to ask him a question, something she said she needed to know. I had put off asking for a while. But Lisa was getting impatient, and I was running out of excuses for not getting around to it. I nudged him with my foot.

"Ian, do you have a girlfriend at school?"

Ian shrugged and looked down at his book.

I thought he was going to leave it at that, and I was almost sorry I'd asked, but then he leaned his back against the wall and started signing.

"There's this girl, Alexia. She moved here last year. I don't really know her that well. But I like her." Ian smiled.

"What's she like?" I asked, putting down my pencil and wrapping my arms around my knees.

"She moved here from California. She's very nice, very sweet." He emphasized the sign for sweet, as if that was her most important attribute. He hesitated. *"And she's really pretty. She has long curly hair and she's always smiling."*

"So?"

"So what?"

"You know, is she going to be your girlfriend?"

Ian shrugged again. *"I don't know. I'm too shy to do anything about it."*

I had to laugh at that. Ian, too shy? *"You're kidding."*

"No, I get all awkward around her." Ian signed "awkward" as if he were a clown.

"You're crazy," I signed. *"Aren't you running the poetry show at your school next week?"*

"What do poetry and girls have to do with each other?" Ian laughed. He leaned back on one elbow and signed with the opposite hand. *"Are you coming to the poetry night?"*

I nodded. *"Sure, since Mom and Dad are going."*

"Yeah, that'll be interesting." Ian rolled his eyes.

"Why?"

"The poems won't be interpreted. Signing only. I don't know how they'll feel about that."

I rested my chin on my knees. My parents were proud of Ian for helping to organize the poetry night at his school; they felt like he was putting his energy into positive things now instead of dwelling on all the bad stuff going on at Hawthorne.

But here was Ian, saying he was worried about my parents, and I knew why. Events at Hawthorne came up a couple of times a year, and whenever they did, we both watched our parents for their reaction. Would they try to talk with the other Deaf students and teachers? Or would they shrink back? I knew Ian wanted them to meet the people who were so important to him, but more often than not they kept to themselves and apologized to Ian later, explaining that they couldn't sign well enough to keep up with the conversations. Now Ian was leading an event that he knew could make them feel even more like strangers in their own son's school, the world he was desperate not to lose. What would that be like for them?

"Don't worry about them. They're really excited for you." I said, knowing at least that was true.

Ian looked at me for a moment. I thought he was going to say something else about our parents, but he didn't. *"I think you'll have a good time."* He paused. *"I'm glad you're going to be there."*

We worked for a while longer, until I heard the doorbell ring. *"Lisa's here,"* I told Ian, and ran downstairs to meet her.

Lisa walked into the house with her usual load of necessary things and we carried them up to my room. Ian was piling up his books and papers when we walked in. He smiled at Lisa and left, saying he was going to finish up his work in his own room. Lisa stared after him.

"I finally asked him," I said, more to break the trance than to share any real information. "You know, if he has a girlfriend."

"Really? What did he say?" Lisa sat on my bed, bouncing up and down.

"He likes someone."

"Oh." Lisa pouted, the same way she did when she heard Marcus Moore was engaged to another tennis player, making a dent, but only a dent, in her fantasy of marrying him herself. "Oh, well," she said, and shrugged. "Things could always change!" She made it sound like she didn't really care, but I could see that she was disappointed.

I shook my head. "You are one wacky woman," I said.

"Why?" she asked, lying down on my bed.

"It would be very weird if you were my best friend and Ian's girlfriend."

"Why?" she asked again. "It would be perfect. All of my interests in one house. Very convenient." She rolled over on her side and looked at me. "So what's her name?"

I told her what I knew about Alexia. After a few minutes the doorbell rang again, putting an end to the conversation. That was okay with me.

This time it was the pizza Ian and I had ordered. My parents were out to a movie and dinner with friends. The three of us sat at the kitchen table and ate together, talking. Ian told us about the trouble his friend Mario had gotten into, teaching sign language at an elementary school near Hawthorne.

"All he taught them were signs for desserts..." Ian laughed. *"He went there every week for ten weeks. Our teacher said he was irresponsible."*

Lisa laughed. *"Yeah, but maybe now the kids will want to learn more sign. They probably like knowing how to say 'I want a cookie.' They can use it in the real world,"* she signed. Lisa helped herself to a second slice of pizza, and the cheese nearly slipped back into the box.

"That's true. I'd rather know that than how to sign I love you." Ian exaggerated the signs for "I love you," as if he were Romeo looking up at Juliet. I watched Ian and Lisa as they chatted about Mario's exploits. Lisa's signing had really improved; it was less choppy now, more natural. When she didn't know a sign, Ian would guess, and they'd somehow figure it out. They hardly ever asked me for help anymore.

After dinner we all sat on the couch in the den and watched an old movie on TV, *King Kong.* As always, captions appeared on the bottom of the screen, but *King Kong* was the kind of movie Ian could have understood even without all the spoken words typed out in front of him. After the movie was over, Ian and Lisa pretended he was the huge ape and she the damsel in distress. Then they switched roles. In a few minutes we were all in hysterics. Ian made a pretty good damsel.

Lisa collapsed on the couch, but then sat straight up. *"Oh, I got some new music today; I want to play it for you,"* she signed. I thought she was talking to me, but then I glanced at her and realized she was looking at my brother. Why would Lisa bring music to play for Ian? What in the world was she thinking?

Lisa sprinted up to my room and returned with a CD. She put the disc into the player next to the television set and turned the volume up loud. I covered my ears. "Turn that down!" I shouted.

Lisa shook her head. She and Ian stood next to each other. We could all feel the vibrations of the drums and synthesizers of the hip-hop music through the floor. Lisa started dancing, slowly at first, and I watched as Ian began moving his body to match hers. Before long, he was holding his own, dancing with Lisa like it was something he did everyday.

What became crystal clear at that moment was that my profoundly deaf brother was a far better dancer than me. I knew enough to understand that you could not hear and still enjoy dancing, but it irritated me to no end that Ian could move his body like that, so easily, so smoothly, with rhythm for goodness sakes, when all I could do was practice in front of the mirror. Or sit on the couch. Lisa motioned for me to join them, but when I didn't, she turned back to Ian and kept dancing.

After three songs, I left and went up to my room. Lisa and Ian didn't notice. They danced through the entire album, the loud music blaring through the door to my room, giving me a headache. When the music stopped, I expected Lisa to come upstairs, but she didn't. After a while I opened my door and stepped outside. It was quiet. I walked downstairs, but the den was empty. The clock on the mantle read 11:25. As I stepped on the first stair to go back to my room I looked out the window. The lights were on in the back-yard, and Ian and Lisa were sitting on the grass, talking. The movements of their hands repeated in their shadows.

I went back to my room and got into bed. I seethed as I waited. I couldn't do anything. I didn't want to read. I didn't want to go to sleep. I wanted Lisa to come back inside. She was supposed to be spending the night with me.

The weird thing, the almost ugly thing I realized was that I wasn't just angry; I was jealous. But how could that be? Was I jealous that my brother had stolen away my best friend when she was supposed to be with me? Or was I jealous of Lisa because she was off talking to Ian? I felt like I'd just gotten him back myself. Could I really be jealous of them talking to each other? And what in the world were they talking about?

Whatever the reason, I couldn't let it go. A half hour later, Lisa opened the door and walked in. I think she expected me to be up, flipping through magazines, but I'd turned the light off. I was in my bed, facing the wall, with the covers pulled up.

"Shel?" she whispered. "Are you sleeping?"

I didn't answer. I listened to the rustling sound as Lisa crawled into her sleeping bag. She took a deep breath and let it out. A few minutes later, I quietly turned to look over at her. She was asleep.

5

The ride to Hawthorne the following Friday seemed to stretch on much longer than two hours. As I leaned my head against the window and closed my eyes, I wondered how Ian tolerated two rides like this every week, one to school on Monday and then back again Friday afternoon. Wouldn't it be nice to roll out of bed and go to the high school six blocks away? I sighed at the thought, but I already knew the answer.

I opened my eyes and looked out as the car whizzed by trees lining the highway. The turkey sandwich I'd eaten for dinner felt heavy in my stomach. I regretted not inviting Lisa. If she were with us, we'd be gossiping and the time would fly by. But I'd decided I wanted one Friday night to myself. There wasn't anything wrong with that, was there? Still, I felt guilty. When she'd asked if she could come over, I'd said we were going to Hawthorne and didn't even say why.

My father sped up the long driveway leading to Hawthorne's main entrance. He parked, and the three of us walked into the building, following signs to the auditorium. We knew our way without them, since Ian was in at least two shows a year at the school. Just this past fall, he'd acted the part of the narrator in *Our Town*, and last year, he was Sky

Masterson in *Guys and Dolls*. That had been interesting. The director had transformed the musical into a choreography of sign language. He kept the characters the same though, and it had been fun to see Ian in the lead part of gambler and romantic, wearing a white suit and matching felt hat.

There were only a few other people in the area outside the auditorium. "Where is everyone?" Dad said, hands on his hips. He walked up to a woman in a black coat and said, "Excuse me."

The woman turned towards him, but then pointed to her ear.

"Oh, um," my father hesitated, as he pulled off his gloves. "What time does the show start?" he asked in sign.

"Six-thirty," the woman answered.

"Thank you," my dad replied. He walked back to us. "Didn't Ian say it started at 6:00?" he asked my mother. Dad doesn't like to wait. He's always on time for everything, and expects everyone else to be too.

"I thought so," Mom said and shrugged, unbuttoning her coat. "We must have misunderstood him." My mother, after working in a doctor's office, is an expert at waiting. She waits for doctors, waits for tests, waits for kids to stick out their tongues. In contrast to my father, already pacing back and forth in front of the door, she is the picture of patience and calm. Waiting time is wasted time in his mind. That fact that I'm almost always late drives him crazy.

"I could really use something to drink," Mom said. "Let's see if we can find a soda machine or something."

She took hold of his arm and they started walking towards the stairs. They turned back to me. "You coming, Shel?" Dad asked.

"No, I'm going to stay here. I want to look at the pictures."

They left, and I wandered over to the long wall across the auditorium's entrance, the school's 'Wall of Pride.' Every time we visit Hawthorne, I find myself drawn to this spot. I start at one end and slowly walk along the wall, studying what seems like a hundred framed posters and pictures. Some of the names I know well, like Beethoven, Thomas Edison and Helen Keller, because I've learned about them in school. I hadn't known, though, that Edison had been deaf. I read about Laurent Clerc, the Deaf teacher who started the first school for Deaf children in America. Douglas Tilden had been a sculptor. In 1988, I. King Jordan became the first Deaf president of Gallaudet University in Washington, D.C.; Ian talked about going there for college. Phyllis Freilich and Bernard Bragg, actors. Patrick Graybill, poet. CJ Jones, comedian. Evelyn Glennie, percussionist. I walked by athletes, reporters, scientists, lawyers, and an accountant. I counted twelve teachers. Some of the posters contained very old black and white pictures. A few, pictures of the television stars, were carefully clipped from magazines and framed. My favorites are the photographs with typed captions underneath. Those are the Hawthorne graduates. I read about a pediatrician, a veterinarian, a secretary, and a seamstress. One man wrote about working at a printing press for thirty years. Two people worked as advocates, and their cards described the rights they protected in their jobs. Several wrote about staying at home to take care of their kids. For as long as he had been coming to Hawthorne, I had always imagined Ian's grown-up photograph on this wall, and wondered what his caption would say.

I heard footsteps behind me, and turned to see my parents returning with sodas in hand. I had been so lost in looking at the photographs that I hadn't noticed the hallway fill up with parents and students, milling about as they waited for the auditorium doors to open. Dad offered me his soda and I took it. The root beer tasted cold and sweet as I quickly drained the rest of the can.

"Any minute now," he said, looking at his watch.

"Sit as close to the front as you can," I said. "I want to be able to see everything." I thought for a moment, and added, "Ian said the poems aren't going to be interpreted."

"Why is that?" my mother asked.

I shrugged. "I didn't ask him. But if I can't listen to the poems, I have to make sure I can see them."

My mother reached over and put her arm around my shoulders, pulling me close into a hug. "It's so good to see you and Ian spending time together again," she said.

I nodded, even as I wriggled a bit. My mom is into spontaneous public shows of affection. I'm more of an in-the-comfort-of-your-own-home sort of girl.

"Excuse me, are you Ian's parents?" a woman's voice asked.

Behind us stood a tall, thin man, and next to him was a woman dressed in black, his interpreter.

"Yes, we're Ian's parents," my mother said and signed.

"It's a pleasure to meet you both," the woman said as the man signed. *"I'm Jared Kennelly, Ian's history teacher. This is Jacqueline, one of our staff interpreters. Do you have a moment?"*

My parents nodded, and Mr. Kennelly continued. I made sure to look at him as he signed, even as I listened to the interpreter's voice. When I was younger, I would always look at the interpreter, until once when Ian told me that it was rude not to look at the person who was actually talking to me. I hated having him point out what I was doing wrong, when I never even realized there was a right or wrong to begin with. Now, though, I was glad he'd told me, and I understood the difference between the person who had something to say, and the person saying it.

"I've gotten to know Ian well over the past few months," Mr. Kennelly began, *"and we've talked a great deal about the possibility of Hawthorne closing. Ian is very concerned that he might have to attend your local high school next year."*

"Yes, we know. We're concerned about it, too," Dad said.

"I want to make sure you're aware of another option, a mainstream program about forty-five minutes from your home. A group of Deaf students attend a public high school in Emerson. It's not a large program, but it's a solid one, with good teachers and interpreters. I encourage you to go visit and see what you think."

"How likely do you think it is, the school closing?" Mom asked quietly.

Mr. Kennelly hesitated and sighed. *"No one knows for sure, but it doesn't look good. We need to begin to prepare. Then, if somehow it doesn't happen..."* But it was clear to us all from the dejected look on his face that he thought it would.

My parents thanked Mr. Kennelly, and he wrote the name of the program on a slip of paper my mother pulled out of her purse. Then they all shook hands, and Mr. Kennelly moved on to another family.

There was some commotion as the doors to the auditorium opened and everyone moved through them to find seats. My parents and I settled into the fifth row. Everywhere around us, people were signing. Whether it was to the person next to them, someone across the aisle or a friend across the auditorium, countless conversations were happening simultaneously. I recognized a couple of other parents we knew through Ian's friends. As I was looking around, I saw Mario's father walking up to us.

"Hey, how are you all?" he asked, extending his hand.

Dad stood up and gave him a hearty handshake. "Good. How are you doing?" he asked.

Mr. Torino shrugged. "We're okay." His face turned serious. "But I don't know about Mario. That boy's got some temper. If they really do close this place, I don't know what he'll do."

Mom nodded. "Same here. I don't know what any of us will do."

Dad let out a heavy sigh. "Did you talk to Mr. Kennelly?" he asked.

Mr. Torino nodded. "That program is an hour and a half away from us. Too far. But we'll look around. Something will have to work out."

The lights flashed once, letting people know it was time to take their seats.

Dad clapped Mr. Torino on the back. "Keep in touch."

"Absolutely," he said, and then they shook hands again, and Mr. Torino went back to his seat.

Mom opened her purse and looked at the slip of paper again. "I'll call Monday," she said to no one in particular. Then she placed it back inside.

The lights flashed again, letting the audience know the show was about to begin. Everyone sat down and a few moments later, Mario, Ian and Nya, a girl Ian had known since he started at Hawthorne, walked out onto the stage. Ian and Nya held back a bit, and Mario, his strawberry blond hair frizzy and wild, sauntered to the center of the stage and addressed the audience. An interpreter in the front row voiced what Mario signed.

"Welcome! Tonight we will perform Hawthorne School for the Deaf's first American Sign Language Poetry Night."

The audience applauded. Some people clapped, but most waved their hands in the air. Applause in the Deaf community needs to be seen, not heard. When the hands had gone down, Mario continued:

"This evening was influenced by the great ASL poet, Clayton Valli. When we decided to organize a poetry night, we got together and read about Clayton Valli's work, and watched his poems. Clayton Valli died in 2003, but in his brief but important life, he developed a deep understanding of American Sign Language poetry and left behind a beautiful collection of his own poems, as well as a great deal of research and information."

Mario stepped back as Nya moved forward. *"We tried to figure out how to help you understand ASL poetry through Clayton Valli's eyes,"* she explained. *"The best way is to show you."*

Ian stepped to the front of the stage. I heard my mother breathe in sharply next to me. I understood why. Ian stood tall and at ease, even with at least a hundred people in the audience. He looked so confident. He looked so grown up.

"Right now, the interpreter is here, but in a moment, we're going to send her away." Ian looked towards the interpreter sitting in the front row and waved goodbye to her, and a ripple of laughter floated up from the audience. *"Why are we doing that? Clayton Valli taught us that poems in American Sign Language should be seen for themselves, without the influence of other languages. We hope you will sit back, relax, and allow the beauty of these poems to reach you. A rhyme in ASL poetry may mean that signs are forming a pattern, or that hand shapes repeat throughout. You may not understand a poem the first time you see it, just as we would read a poem several times in English to understand its meaning. That's okay. We are here tonight to celebrate the beauty of our language, and to share it with you. Sit back. Relax. Welcome."*

With that, Ian nodded his head towards the interpreter, and she placed her microphone in a stand and took a seat in the audience. He then held out his hand, and a little girl walked slowly onto the stage. She looked like she couldn't have been older than eight or nine. She introduced herself, the fingers of her right hand carefully forming the letters of her name. Ciara. She showed us her sign name as Ian inched back into the darkness.

Ciara took a breath and began her poem. It was a poem about a tree, and at the end I realized her hands had kept the shape of the number five throughout. The tree stood tall and strong, and its leaves gently fell and blew in the wind. It was lovely, and the audience's applause went on and on. Ciara looked so proud.

Many more kids followed and signed poems that they'd created, and others that Clayton Valli had performed. There was one about a mushroom, one about a snowflake, and one about a cow and a dog. One was titled "Deaf World." There were many I couldn't understand, but it didn't matter. If I was lost, I watched the person, the feeling in their face and their body. Nya looked like a ballerina as her hands moved. When it was Mario's turn, he performed a poem of his own about a residential school closing, and in it, he said goodbye to everything dear to him. At the end though, he leapt up and shouted and signed *"No!"* with so much anger and power that everyone in the audience was startled, and it took a moment for anyone to remember to applaud.

Ian's poem was last. He performed one of Clayton Valli's, called "Dandelion." Ian switched back and forth from the flowers to the angry man trying to mow them down. His body became the delicate dandelion, its petals opening to the sun during the day and closing at night, until it turns to puffy white. Its seedlings float off in the wind. The man sees it and grabs it by the stem, and its seeds scatter all around, in spite of him. How can I explain how beautiful the poem was? I'd have to be a poet.

I looked over at Mom and Dad after the applause for Ian died down. Ian and I could not have been more wrong when we'd worried about their reaction. They were beaming. Tears ran down my mother's cheeks and she wiped them away with the back of her hand.

Mario stepped forward and addressed the audience. The interpreter stepped up to the microphone.

"Tonight's performance was the first at Hawthorne, but it won't be the last. Hawthorne has given us many gifts. Education. Confidence. Pride. Experience. I grew up watching older kids, learning from older kids who showed me that I could do whatever I wanted to do. Now, Ciara and the other kids just starting out look to me and my friends. They see how much we enjoy our language, our culture and our community. You don't teach that: you live it. People very far away and with very little understanding about us are making decisions that will affect all of our lives. We will not let that happen. You saw the last poem. We are like the dandelion. We are gentle and beautiful and resilient. The dandelion is not easily picked, and this school will not easily be shut down."

As Mario finished his speech and his arms fell to his sides, the audience erupted in applause. Everyone was on their feet, and an ocean of hands waved in the air. The performers all came onto the stage and took a bow, and then another, as the ovation continued. Eventually the curtain dropped, and the audience quieted. We shuffled along with the crowd trying to get backstage.

We spotted Ian, and my father squeezed his body between people in order to get to him, grabbing him in a bear hug once he did. My mother joined in, and I stood off to the side, looking at my family's group hug. Ian glanced over at me, and I signed one sign, *cool*. He smiled.

"Wonderful, wonderful," my mother gushed to Ian, signing and speaking at the same time. "How did you put that together?"

Ian grinned. *"We all did. We all worked on it together. It wasn't that hard."*

Mario ran up and hooked his arm around Ian's neck. *"You coming?"* he asked.

"I'm going to go home with Mario for the weekend," Ian told my parents. *"Okay?"*

My parents agreed, and hugged Ian some more. I looked at my watch. We'd be home by ten, after another boring trip with no one to keep me company. I'd counted on Ian for the ride home.

"See you next weekend," Ian said, punching me lightly in the arm.

"Yeah," I answered, annoyed.

"What?" he asked, stopping in front of me, even as Mario pulled at his arm.

"Nothing." I forced a smile. *"Really, nothing."*

"Okay, see you later," he said, but he looked confused.

"See you later," I signed back, and then watched as he was swallowed up by the crowd offering him hugs and pats on the back.

I could have kicked myself. When had I become a giant strip of Velcro, and with my own brother, no less? My cheeks flushed, and my mother even asked if I was feeling all right. I told her I was fine, even though all I wanted to do was disappear.

I slipped away from the crowd and walked back to the Wall of Pride. No one else was around, and I scanned the pictures again. Something about them calmed me down, made me stop beating myself up for feeling disappointed.

But as I stood there, I suddenly realized something else. It hit me like a snowball thrown right at my face. Sometime soon, all these pictures I had stared at for so many years might have to come down. They'd be packed up, along with everything else at Hawthorne. No one would see Ian's picture, or anyone else's for that matter. I softly bumped my shoe against the wall. I had understood what Ian was afraid of losing before, but only as an idea. As I stared at the photos, I finally felt it.

I rode the two hours home without saying anything. My parents, on the other hand, didn't stop talking. I was glad for Ian. He couldn't have given them a better example for why Hawthorne needed to stay open. It was like a dim light bulb had suddenly brightened. They had always understood that Hawthorne was so important to him. Now they had the words to explain why.

The phone was ringing as we entered the house.

"That's got to be Lisa," Mom said. "Who else calls at this hour?" She grabbed the phone as it rang for the fourth time. I heard her say hello as I peeled off my jacket and hung it in the hall closet.

"Is it Lisa?" I called out, but Mom had her back to me.

"Apparently not," I said to my father, and he chuckled.

Mom was speaking in hushed tones, and I suddenly felt a chill go up my back. When had I felt that way before? I looked over at her, standing with her shoulders hunched, her hand clutching the doorframe. Her voice had sounded the same way when the hospital called to say that Grandma had had another stroke.

"Something's wrong," I whispered, and I could see from my father's face that he knew it too. My mother hung up the phone and slumped into a chair in the kitchen.

"Karen?" my father said, hurrying to her.

I followed my father into the kitchen. Mom's face was pale and she was shaking. "Shelly, honey, sit down," she told me in a quiet voice.

I sunk into the chair across from hers. I will always remember that moment, the moment before she told me.

I think it was my last precious moment of being a kid. In the next breath, she quietly told me that Lisa had been hit by a car, an accident while she was walking her dog. It had happened very quickly. Lisa had died.

My mother reached over to take my hand, but for some reason, I pulled it back. I stared at her, and for a split second I wondered why she would say such a terrible thing to me. Her words repeated in my head and I tried to shake them off, to wake up, and be anywhere but there. What had she said?

Lisa is dead. Lisa is dead.

My breath came fast, and I felt like I might throw up. How could it be true? My father, standing behind me, put his hands on my shoulders. No, there had to be a mistake. Someone else had been walking Ruby. Someone else had been hit. Not Lisa.

Mom was crying. She wiped her eyes with her sleeve. Her nose was red. "That was Macie's mother," she said. "The girls are at their house. They thought it would help to be together."

It started with my hands, and soon my whole body was shaking. I realized that I was screaming – not words, just sounds that I had never made or heard before. Dad held me. When I stopped, he kept hold of me, patting my hair and speaking to me in a quiet, soothing way. I don't remember what he said. I don't remember anything.

My parents drove me to Macie's house and stayed to talk to her parents in the living room. Macie, Catherine and I sat on the floor of Macie's bedroom. I was numb. I felt the way you feel when you haven't slept all night, all foggy and confused. Drops of blood dotted Catherine's shirt. She always gets a bloody nose when she cries. Macie leaned her head on the bed. "Why did it happen? Why did it happen?" she said out loud, but neither of us answered her.

Catherine couldn't stop crying; Macie didn't cry at all. They kept talking about Lisa and the accident. Everything they said made it worse, forced me to draw a picture in my head when I wanted my mind to stay blank. I did not want to imagine a car or a dog or anything else. All I wanted to do was to get out of there.

Don't get me wrong, I love them both. I do. But I was suffocating in that room, where a million times before there had been four of us on the floor.

I called down to my parents and asked them to take me home.

I stared out the window as my father drove. Mom told me what was going to happen next. The funeral would be on Sunday. I could hear her talking, but I only really heard two words. Funeral Sunday. When we got home, my mother asked if I wanted to sleep with her, but I said no. I wanted to be in my own bed; I wanted the noise in my head to stop.

I lay in my bed, in the dark. The window was open a few inches, and a warm wind blew in. I pulled the blankets up to my neck even though it wasn't cold. How could it be that she was no longer alive? How could it be? Just last week, she was here, next to me. How could I be lying in this bed, breathing, when she was dead? My head ached with all the questions that raced through it. And the biggest question, boiled down to one word, burst like a lightning bolt over and over in my brain. If…if…if.

Somehow I fell asleep, but woke with a start every few hours, and each time, I remembered my mother's words and heard them again as if I were hearing them for the first time. As the first light of dawn crept in through my window, I flipped over onto my side, then sat up, startled.

Someone was asleep on the floor beside my bed.

For a second, I thought it was Lisa. I had finally woken up from a terrible dream. Then I realized that it was not Lisa, but Ian, asleep in his sleeping bag. My parents must have called him at Mario's, and he'd come home so that I wouldn't be alone. The pain rushed at me again, filling every part of my body, but this time I felt something else, too.

Yesterday, if someone had told me you could be filled to the brim with feelings of love and grief, all at the same time, I wouldn't have believed them.

Now I understood.

6

The funeral took place two days later.
People spoke, and cried, but I can't remember any of
what they said. My parents and Ian stayed by me the whole
time. Hundreds of people were there. But nothing made
sense to me; everything seemed to be happening around me
as if I were underwater, watching.

Macie and Catherine sat with us during the service and
stood next to me at the cemetery. So many people were
there that I could barely see anything, but I didn't want to
see, so it was okay. Ian and I hardly spoke to each other, but
I found that comforting. He simply stayed close. There was
nothing anyone said to me that felt the least bit helpful. It
was better to say nothing at all.

Afterwards, people went back to Lisa's house to sit *shiva*
with her family. Macie's mother asked me what that meant,
and I explained that it was a Jewish custom of spending
time with the family the week after someone died, so they
wouldn't be alone. Macie stared blankly at my shoes while
I spoke. She seemed to be swaying slightly, back and forth,
as if she might fall any second. Her mother put her arm
around her shoulder, and said they would see me there, but
I shook my head.

"I can't do it," I said. "I can't. I'm sorry."

I walked to the car and waited there for Ian and my parents, who were talking to Macie and her mother. When they returned to the car, we all got in and drove home, no questions asked. I was relieved. I couldn't bear to see the inside of Lisa's house yet, not when I could still hear her voice singing inside my head.

Back home, I went up to my room and closed the door. Then I went through every piece of clothing I owned, every notebook, every drawer, looking for notes from Lisa. We had written notes to each other all day long, passing them back and forth in the halls at school and across aisles in class.

Slowly, a pile of crumpled and folded papers built up on my bed. I found a note about Mr. You-Know-Who in my jacket pocket. There were more at the bottom of my backpack. On the back page of my history notebook from eighth grade, Lisa had practiced signing the name she'd take after she married tennis star Marcus Moore. Lisa Meyer Moore. At the time, I had told her it made me think of hotdogs. She didn't care, and filled the page with her new signature.

I came across a bunch of photographs I'd taken with a new camera: Lisa posing with each of my stuffed animals. Where were the others? There had to be more. I dumped my desk drawers upside down on the floor, and sifted through the contents. I found letters from camp, and postcards from her trip to England. I found old poems I'd written, with her comments scrawled on the edges. Alongside one she'd written, "I love it! You should send this to a magazine."

I smoothed out each one and carefully stacked the precious pages. This was all I had. This was all I had left of my best friend.

7

Over the next few days, I went to school because I had to go. While I was there, I did whatever I could to avoid looking over at Lisa's chair in homeroom, or in English, and I ate lunch alone outside on the bleachers, without telling anyone. Sandoval Jones stopped by my locker one afternoon as I was dragging my books out. Without Lisa to share him with, though, he was no longer Mr. You-Know-Who, but just another person I couldn't bear talking to.

As soon as school was over, I'd run home and crawl back in bed. All I wanted to do was to do nothing. My parents brought me food, and tried to talk to me, but everything everyone said felt like needles poking into my skin. Macie and Catherine called, and I would talk for a few minutes and hang up, telling them I'd call them later. But I didn't call. There was nothing to say.

When Ian came home on Friday evening, he ate dinner with my parents in the kitchen while I picked at my chicken, still in bed.

After dinner Ian came upstairs and stood in my doorway. I didn't say anything, so he walked in and sat at the edge of my bed.

"You should write down things you remember about her," he said. *"It will help you later."*

"What are you talking about? How do you know?" I asked, and the signs came out harsher than I expected.

"Because that's what I did when Grandma died."

I stared at him. *"Really?"*

He nodded. *"Want to see?"*

"Yes," I signed quietly.

Ian went to his room and came back with a plain red notebook. He sat down on the bed, flipped through the pages until he found what he was looking for, and then handed me the book.

Remember-
  Friday night dinner with the whole family
  the way the house smelled when Grandma baked knishes
  chocolate chip cookies
  licking batter off the spoon
  the one sign Grandma learned really well – eat!
  the sweaters she knitted that always had too many colors
  in them
  chicken soup, stuffed peppers, challah bread
  the quarters she gave us when we were little for soda
  that Mom and Dad didn't want us to drink
  false teeth in a pink cup next to her bed
  her big yellow chair
  playing checkers
  shopping on Nassau Street every Thursday afternoon
  fighting over ice cream at Muddy's with Shelly
  my favorite flavors – mint chocolate chip, fudge brownie,
  rocky road
  flower dresses
  playing hide and seek and hiding under Grandma's bed

I closed the book and put it down on my lap. For a moment, memories of my grandmother swirled around in my head. I could practically taste the knishes, the way the dough wrapped around mashed potato would fall apart in my mouth with each bite. I counted back. Four years without her. When I thought of her now, she was hazy in my mind, but always smiling. I could feel the smile. Ian had brought it back.

Why was I surprised that Ian had written down his memories of our grandmother? He'd refused to go to her funeral, and I hadn't understood why. Of course, my parents forced him to go, and he'd stood on the side as if he was trying to separate himself as much as possible from what was going on. At the time I thought he didn't care enough, but now I saw that he had cared too much.

"Did you ever wear any of those sweaters?" I asked Ian.

He shook his head and made a face. *"No. Did you?"*

"No. But I still have them, in my bottom drawer. I like looking at them sometimes."

He smiled. *"Me too."* He took the notebook back from me. *"Did I forget anything?"*

I shrugged. *"She used to call us to make sure we got home, even though we only lived two miles away. Dad always yelled at her to stop treating him like a baby."*

Ian laughed. *"I remember that."*

I looked at him. *"I didn't think you remembered when we used to have Friday night dinners with all the cousins. That was a long time ago. You missed so many dinners…"* I paused.

"Getting home late from Hawthorne, I know. I missed out on a lot of things. But I would have missed out on other things if I'd stayed here."

"I know," I said, and sighed. Ian and I looked at each other for a few minutes, not saying anything. It felt okay. It made it possible for me to start talking.

"I feel like Lisa was someone who really knew me, and loved me, and now she's gone," I signed, as tears rolled down my face. *"I miss her so much."*

Ian was trying to keep from crying, I could see that. *"She felt the same way about you,"* he said. *"She told me."*

"She did?"

He nodded. *"She said you were the one friend she felt would always be there for her."*

"I don't think that's true. I depended on her."

Ian shook his head. *"No, you depended on each other. She told me. She told me how you helped her deal with her parents being split up, how you listened to her complain all the time when she forgot her stuff at either her mom's or dad's house. She said she got stuck at a terrible tennis camp last summer, and you wrote to her every day. You wrote every day?"*

I nodded this time. For a moment, a small, pleasant feeling crept in where for a week there had only been pain and sadness. I remembered writing to her, having to think of something new to say every day. Sometimes I'd get silly, and list all the foods I'd eaten, or the clothes I'd tossed into the laundry. Most of the time, though, I wrote to her about everything I was thinking. Everything I was feeling. And she wrote back.

"When did she tell you all this?"

"I don't know." Ian shrugged. *"She told me a lot that night we danced. Do you remember? We went outside because she wanted to talk to me about you."*

The bitter memory of that night came rushing back at me, like a big wave at the ocean that pulls you under. *"What? What do you mean? What did she say?"*

He hesitated, looking at me carefully. *"It bothered her that you didn't dance with us, that it seemed like you couldn't. She wanted to know how to help you... relax. Stop worrying so much. She wanted you to see yourself like we see you."* Ian grabbed hold of my hand. *"She loved you very much."*

Suddenly I felt like I couldn't breathe. I started crying harder than I had since I'd first heard my mother's terrible words. My chest heaved and hurt from every painful feeling that I felt in my heart. Ian cried too. He reached over and held me, and I leaned into his chest. We cried together on my bed for a long time.

After a while, I stopped. I felt numb, empty. Most of all, I was very tired. Ian leaned over and grabbed a few tissues off my nightstand. He made a trumpet noise as he blew his nose, and I surprised myself by smiling.

"What?" he asked.

"Nothing. Silly stuff. You sounded like an elephant."

Ian smiled. *"Thank you for teaching me what an elephant sounds like."*

I knew it would make me cry again, but I had to say it. *"I love you, Ian."*

"I love you, too," he echoed, and put his hand on my shoulder. I suddenly felt like I had to tell someone, that I could not hold onto my secret any longer.

"But..." I shook my head.

"What?"

My hands and arms shook as if they'd suddenly turned to rubber. They barely dared to form the signs. *"Ian, it's my fault."*

"What?" Ian signed crisply. *"What are you talking about?"*

"It's my fault. It's because of me. If I'd invited her to poetry night she wouldn't have died. She would have been with us. If I'd invited her..."

Ian stared at me without moving for a few seconds. I could almost see his thoughts move through his brain like trains running along a track. Would he hate me now? Lisa had become his friend, too. Would he simply get up and walk away?

Ian took a deep breath that filled his chest, and shook his head. *"Listen to me. Are you listening?"* He asked, and waited until I nodded my head. *"If there wasn't a poetry night. If the person driving had taken a different street. If her mother had walked the dog."* He leaned in close and raised his eyebrows. *"Do you blame her mother?"*

I shook my head no.

"No. Of course you don't. None of these things matter. A million different things could have happened, but only one thing did happen. An accident. No one's fault. Definitely not yours. The worst accident possible."

I stared into Ian's eyes, seeing for the first time how much he looked like my father. I nodded my head gently.

"Sometimes I just can't believe it," I told him. *"But I know it's true, because I can feel it here."* I put my hand on my chest. There'd been a constant ache there for a week.

Ian nodded. *"On the bus home this afternoon, I forgot for a minute. I thought, maybe Lisa will sleep over and we'll watch a movie."* He looked out the window, and then back at me. *"I feel lucky that I got to know her. I could have easily missed knowing her at all."*

Ian ran his hand through his hair. *"You're going to think this is crazy, but I feel the same way about you."*

"Why would you say that?"

"All week in school, I thought about Lisa, and how great she was. I thought about how you were best friends. And then I realized that until a few months ago, I'd barely said two words to her, and hardly more to you, either. I was always so angry."

"About Hawthorne?" I asked, expecting him to nod in return.

He shook his head. *"No, not just Hawthorne. It started a long time before anyone ever thought about closing Hawthorne."* Ian took a breath. *"You seemed to have it so easy. School a few blocks away, friends a few blocks away. Mom and dad to yourself, and you all got along. I guess I wanted what you had, just my version of it… So I pushed you away. I knew I was doing it. I feel bad about it now. I wanted to be at Hawthorne, but at the same time… And then we had that fight, and everything changed. I don't know why, but it was like something shook me and I woke up. I let myself get to know you again. It would have been so easy for things to stay the same."*

I had to smile. *"Well, just so you know, I always thought you were the one who had it easy."*

Ian looked at me as if I'd just told him my hair was blue.

"No, really. You had so many friends, and you loved your school. You always seemed so sure of yourself, when I didn't have a clue. And anyway, I fight with mom and dad too. You just get all the attention when you're around."

His eyes narrowed. *"That's true, isn't it? I get all the attention when I'm around. That must be terrible."*

I thought about my answer for a moment. A few months ago, I would have said 'Yes, it's terrible. I barely exist when you're home.' In fact, I had said just that to Lisa. But I didn't feel that way anymore, especially not now.

"It doesn't matter like it used to. A lot of things don't matter anymore." Suddenly, I knew I wasn't just talking about Ian anymore, but about Lisa, about the pain in my chest, about the gaping hole in my world.

Ian straightened the stuffed animals lining my bed. *"It's going to take a long time. It will take a long time to feel better, but you will. Or at least, you'll feel better than this. And you'll do the things you like to do again. But,"* Ian hesitated, *"don't let it pull you down, the way I let being angry pull me away."*

Ian leaned back against the wall. *"And anyway, it's not what Lisa would have wanted. She would want you to think about her, but to keep on living, to keep on being part of life. Do you understand?"*

"Yes," I answered. And I did, but more importantly, Ian had given me something to hang onto, a rope to pull me out of the swirling sea. He was right. I knew what Lisa would want me to do. It was something I could hold onto, something else I still had.

That night I slept through to morning for the first time in a week. I ate breakfast with my family. After lunch, Ian tapped me on the shoulder and said he felt like getting some ice cream. We trekked up to Nassau Street, mostly in silence, and went to Muddy's. We bought two pints of ice cream, fudge brownie and praline swirl, and ate them on the walk back home.

8

The next day I brought Lisa's mother a basket of banana muffins I'd baked that morning. Gwen met me at the door, and hugged me tightly. I was shocked by my first look at her when she let me go. Gwen had her hair pulled back, and there were dark circles under her eyes. Her face was pale. She looked so much older than she'd ever looked before.

Gwen took my hand and we walked together into the kitchen. The orange kitchen. Not pastel orange, like sherbet, but bold, in-your-face orange, like, well, freshly squeezed juice. Lisa couldn't stand the color, and she would mock it every chance she got. She called her kitchen the Tropicana Lounge. I sat down at the round table in the center of the room, as Gwen poured tea into two cups.

"I'm sorry I didn't come last week," I said, as she leaned over me.

She waved her hand. "That's okay. I didn't want to be here either." She sat down and poured sugar into her tea. She stirred it with a spoon. "People were here all day. It felt so claustrophobic. There was someone in the house all the time, until late at night. I barely knew some of the people who came by."

"That must have been hard."

Gwen stared at her cup. "It was hard with them, and it's hard without them," she said quietly.

I sipped my tea, not knowing what to say.

"I see why people do it though. The *shiva*. I heard stories about Lisa I would probably never have heard otherwise. And people talked about other things too, baseball and movies and the new restaurant opening in town. It made the time pass. Seven days." She sipped her tea.

Gwen leaned her head into her hand and looked at me. Suddenly, she looked like a little girl. "The thing I keep thinking is, she was happy, right? She crammed a whole lot of happiness into fifteen years."

"She was definitely happy," I said. "I mean, she was a regular person and all, but she always had a way of making things fun."

Gwen nodded. "I always felt that way too. That was her gift. I think everyone has one, and that was hers."

I thought about that for a moment. Did everyone have a gift? Lisa certainly did, Gwen was right about that. If Lisa was around, something was going to happen. There was going to be music, or dancing. And she could turn it off if she had to; she could listen, she was a great friend. So how does someone like that get hit by a car and die?

I didn't say any of this out loud. Instead, Gwen and I talked about being back in school, and how Lisa's friends were doing. I told her there had been counselors around all week long, letting kids know they could talk to them if they wanted to.

"Did you go?" Gwen asked.

I shook my head. "No. I mean, at least, not yet."

Gwen sat back in her chair. "It's not a bad thing. I'm going to go see someone next week."

"But…" I started, and then stopped.

"What?"

"Don't you think it'll be weird talking about Lisa to someone who never knew her?"

She shrugged. "I don't think so. Actually, you might think this is strange, but I think it's easier to talk about her to someone who didn't know her. We're all so overwhelmed by how we feel." She reached over and touched my arm. "But it's not hard to talk to you. I'm so glad you came."

We sat together a while longer, and then I said I needed to go home to help my mother with something. I knew it was the right thing to do.

On Monday, I sat with Macie and Catherine at lunch. I felt stronger, and didn't think I would burst into tears the minute I sat down at the table. It wasn't like it had been before, and I hadn't expected it to be, but our conversation felt awkward and weird. Like we were all wondering what we should say next. Half the time we chewed on our sandwiches, instead of leaving them half-finished because we didn't have enough time to talk and eat. On Tuesday, I went back to eating in the bleachers.

On Wednesday, when Miss James, the school counselor, waved at me on my way to English, I asked her if she had a few minutes to talk. I'd decided Gwen had a point, and that maybe someone who didn't know Lisa so well could help me. I was determined not to cry, but to talk about Macie and Catherine. I wanted to know how to be comfortable around them again. Instead, I cried for an hour, as I told her story after story about Lisa. And the strangest thing happened. In the middle of one of my stories, my nose running so much that I'd filled the wastebasket with balls of tissue, I suddenly started to sign. I didn't notice it at first, and once I did, I stopped. But for a few minutes, I was signing to Miss James. She didn't say anything about it. But she listened to me for the whole hour in a careful kind of way, and when I left I felt drained. Still, I knew I'd go back. I was like a balloon, blown too big, and now some of the air had been let out.

By Friday I had made it through almost two days without crying, and I thought that maybe I'd figured out a way to hold myself together. So I wasn't prepared at all when I lost it in Social Studies.

Every year, Mr. Polin gives a presentation for the ninth grade class he teaches. He talks about his service during the Viet Nam war, and shows his slides. It was dark in the room. Mr. Polin explained the circumstances of the war, and I found my mind drifting. But then he started talking about the people he served with, and slide after slide showed some of the men he'd known. He told us their names, and then he told us when and where they had been killed. And that was it. I started crying, my head in my hands, and the next thing I knew, Sandoval Jones was kneeling by my desk, patting my back. Mr. Polin turned off the machine and switched on the lights. Later, I realized I wasn't the only one crying. Mr. Polin came over and squeezed my hand, and then walked over to the front of the room.

"I think we all need to talk," he said, in a voice that was soft and quiet, and he motioned for all of us to come and sit on the floor. We did. Sandoval sat next to me, and the class made a circle.

"I wasn't sure if this was the time to show you the slides," Mr. Polin began speaking slowly. "I almost didn't. But maybe we needed them to talk about what's happened. Lisa was a member of this class. She was one of us. I find it very hard to believe she won't be back."

At first, everyone sat in silence. I think we were all waiting for someone to be the first person to talk.

"That girl always made me laugh so hard," Nakeesha said, hugging her knees.

"She was always like that," Bryan added. "I knew her back in kindergarten."

Slowly, everyone started saying something about Lisa. Some people shared something they remembered, something funny she did or said, and some people talked about how they felt now that she was gone. Most of us were crying. Mr. Polin made comments and nodded when people talked.

"I just met her this year," Assaf said, his chin leaning on his knees. "It was the first day of English, and we had to do some kind of warm-up exercise. You know, to get to know each other. And she did this hysterical Star Trek routine. I couldn't stop laughing. She was just too funny. Too smart."

Seneca Hale wiped her eyes on her sleeve. "I was so jealous of her. I was always so competitive with her," she said.

I have to admit, my opinion of Seneca moved up a few notches at that moment. She'd been honest, and it wasn't pretty. I appreciated that.

"I liked her," was all Sandoval quietly said. I stared at him, shocked. He'd said it in front of the whole class, but I might have been the only one who knew what he meant. Sandoval liked Lisa. All those months of thinking about him, and it turned out he was thinking about her, too.

The bell rang, signaling the end of class, and we slowly stood up and shuffled out the door. Sandoval came up to me and quietly said, "I have something for you", but then he quickly moved past me through the door. I looked over at Mr. Polin as he put his hand on my shoulder.

"Miss Marks, the door to this classroom will always be open to you," he said, back to his automated voice. But it was just the right thing to say, and I knew he meant it.

9

"You hiding?"

I shielded my eyes from the sun with my hand, and looked up to see Sandoval, holding a lunch tray. Was I hiding? And more importantly, why was Sandoval asking?

"I don't know," I said. "Maybe."

"Okay if I sit with you?"

I nodded, and Sandoval sat down next to me. We were at the top of the bleachers, looking down at an 11th grade gym class making a lame attempt at a two-mile run.

"I can't believe they'll be making us do that run until we graduate from here," he said, taking a bite of his pizza.

"Tell me about it," I agreed.

We sat without saying anything else for a few minutes. The thing is, they weren't awkward-silence minutes, just quiet minutes, where we ate and didn't talk. In the old days, a whole month ago, if Sandoval had looked at me, much less sat down next to me, my stomach would have been in knots. My hands would have started sweating, my brain scrambling for something funny to say. I would have ended up with a stomach ache, a headache, and nightmares where I'd replay every wrong thing I'd said. Now though, with a real nightmare to deal with, all of that was gone. Not only that, but sitting with Sandoval actually felt good. Calm. It was nice to have the company.

"So I told you I had something for you," he said, and reached into his backpack. He pulled out a package wrapped in green tissue paper and handed it to me.

I held a small, rectangular package on my lap. "Should I open it?" I asked him.

"Yeah." He laughed. "That's what you do with a present, right?"

"Right." I tore open the paper, uncovering a photograph of Lisa and me, just our faces, laughing together. We looked so happy. Sandoval had framed the picture in a simple wooden frame. I could not imagine a more precious gift.

"It's so…" My words caught in my throat, but I wanted him to know how much I needed that photograph. "It's so beautiful. Thank you so much, Sandoval." We stared at it for a few minutes. "I hardly have any pictures of her. None of us together." I ran my finger along the edge of the frame. "I don't remember you taking this."

"Well, you know, I was trying to be discreet," he said, shyly.

Right, I thought, you're not really supposed to let the person you secretly like know you're secretly taking pictures of her. I looked at Sandoval. Here was another person, with a whole different set of 'ifs' tumbling around in his brain. At least I could give him something back.

"She thought you were really great," I said, looking him in the eye. "She really liked you."

He smiled, and then we both looked out to the field. We sat there, watching the stragglers come in from their run, until the bell rang. I held the frame against my chest as I stood up to get my stuff and move to class.

"You're not hanging out with Macie and Catherine any-more?" Sandoval asked, as he put one arm and then the other through the straps of his backpack.

I made a face and looked at him. "I still hang out with them. Why do you say that?"

He shrugged. "It just seems that way."

I let out a long sigh. "Yeah, well, I just haven't... wanted to have lunch with them right now," I said, slowly. "It's too much."

He nodded. "They miss you, though." He shrugged again, looking at me with the eyes Lisa and I had found so irresistible. Now, they seemed sincere, kind. He wasn't tell-ing me anything I didn't already know, but the way he said it made me think about it again. And for some reason, I felt like I could talk to Sandoval Jones.

"I want to see them, I do," I said.

Sandoval's eyebrows went up slightly. He was on to me. There was no point in lying, and I didn't want to anyway.

"But I just can't stand being with them," I said. And it was out, the brutal, honest truth.

The bell rang again. The next period was starting, and we would both be late. Sandoval stuck his hands into the pockets of his jeans and rocked on his feet. "Maybe you just can't see them here. But they're your friends. Do something different. You know, go fly a kite or something."

I tilted my head and smirked at him. "Fly a kite?"

"Yeah." He smiled. "I think that'll work. Kite flying. Or bike riding. Go ride around the lake. Then you don't even have to talk or anything. It'll be good."

As it turned out, Sandoval was right. I called Macie that afternoon, and she called Catherine, and we met at the lake and rode our bikes around for two hours. When we were done we were so wiped out we all dropped our bikes and fell on the grass under a tree. We had done something different, something the four of us had never done together. For now, at least, the awkwardness was gone. I could breathe with them again.

Macie rolled onto her stomach. "Is something going on with you and Mr. You-Know-Who?" Macie asked, her head resting on her hands.

I shook my head. "It's not like that. I don't think about him like that anymore," I said.

I didn't add anything about what Sandoval had said about Lisa. It wasn't a secret; after all, he'd said he liked her in front of the whole history class. But still, it didn't seem right.

Catherine picked dandelions and gathered them into a bouquet. "Come have lunch with us tomorrow," she said softly.

I wanted to say yes. I tried to picture myself back at the table, the three of us talking and eating, but it was still too hard.

I shook my head. "I can't. I can't do that yet." I picked a dandelion of my own and held it to my nose. "But I can do this." I handed her the flower. "Okay?"

"Yeah," Catherine answered. Macie smiled and threw some grass at me. And so I knew we were going to be all right.

Sandoval found me on the bleachers during lunch on Tuesday, Wednesday, and again on Thursday. Two days in, he started talking about himself. His parents were divorced. His mother works as a therapist; his father is a musician. He's named after a famous jazz musician, Arturo Sandoval. He has a sister in college somewhere in California. He misses his friends in Washington, where he lived the year before, but he says he's getting used to this school. And another thing: he's allergic to kiwi.

Sandoval showed up late on Friday. In the few moments that ticked by before he arrived, I realized I had a new friend.

10

I held the letter in my hand and dialed my mother's office
number.

"Stanworth Pediatrics. May I help you?"

"Karen Marks, please," I said quickly.

"She's in with a patient right now. Can I have her call
you back?"

"Um, yeah. Tell her Shelly called. Thanks." I hung up
and started punching in the numbers of the car dealership
where my father worked. I was luckier this time. When I told
her who I was, the receptionist asked me to wait a moment,
and then connected me to my dad.

"Shelly? What's up?" he said, and I could hear the concern
in his voice. I don't usually call him at work. I hadn't thought
that he would worry there was something wrong with me.

"Dad, there's a letter here for you from the state. It's got
to be about Hawthorne."

My father was quiet for a moment. "Open it," he said
tersely.

I stuck my finger under the flap and ripped the seam. I
pulled out the folded page and quickly skimmed the letter.

"Shelly?" Dad snapped.

"They're closing the school, Dad. It's closing at the end
of June."

I heard my father let out a deep, heavy sigh on the other end of the phone. All the letters they'd written and calls they'd made to prevent this moment had failed. "Put it away, Shelly. Don't show it to Ian if he gets home before we do. We'll tell him."

I knew I wouldn't be able to do that. I had the pit-of-my-stomach feeling I get when someone tells me to do something that doesn't feel right at all. I understood what my father was thinking, but it didn't matter. That wasn't the kind of secret I could agree to keep.

"I can't do that, Dad." I said it simply, but I heard the strength in my voice. It surprised me as much as it must have surprised him.

My father took a moment to answer. "Okay. I'll come home." And then he said goodbye and hung up, and I carefully folded the letter and put it back in the envelope.

Dad had better luck reaching my mother, and within twenty minutes they were home, even though Ian wasn't due for more than an hour. They read the letter over a few times, and Dad started pacing the living room floor. Mom started cleaning, which is what she does when she's stressed. They were both making me more anxious with every passing minute, so I went upstairs and looked out my window, watching for the bus.

When I was younger, and Ian had first started going to Hawthorne, I would sit by the window every Friday afternoon waiting for him. Depending on traffic and the weather, he could get home as early as five thirty or as late as seven. Sometimes my mother or father had to pull me away from the window. My grandmother would be in the kitchen testing the knishes. The cousins and their parents would arrive and it would be time for Friday night dinner. But I wanted to wait by the window until the bus pulled up and delivered Ian home, too. It didn't felt right without him.

Eventually, the yellow bus pulled up to the house, and Ian ran down the steps, his backpack slung over his shoulder. He started to make his way up the driveway and looked up, spotting me in the window. This would be his before and after moment, I thought. He waved at me and then walked into the house.

I'm not sure what we expected, but I think my parents and I were ready for Ian to do something, to react in some way that would show how he felt about the letter once he'd read it. I know we were each holding our breath, waiting for him to show his rage. Rip up the letter. Kick the wall. I half expected him to pick up the closest object and hurl it through a window. Ian can be that way. But he didn't do any of those things. He simply read the letter and then folded it up and put it back in its envelope. Then he went and sat on the couch, staring at the cell phone in his hands. He started texting. I hovered in the kitchen next to where he was sitting, pretending to do homework.

A full hour went by where no one had said anything to anyone, and all we could hear was the sound of Ian texting away. My father came downstairs, dressed in sweats. "Go get dressed," he said and signed. "Let's play ball."

Ian looked up, his face pale and flat. Then he shrugged his shoulders, and tossed the phone on the couch. He sprinted up the stairs and came back in a t-shirt and shorts. He and my father went out to the basketball hoop at the end of our driveway.

"This ought to be good," Mom said warily. This, meaning basketball, was my father's classic way of going at most problems with Ian. When Ian was younger and things were rough at school, or they had had an argument, he would say the same thing, "Let's play ball," and they'd work it out on our driveway court. But it had been years since the last match-up, and I could tell that Mom doubted whether a game of one-on-one was what Ian needed at that moment.

Mom and I went to the sofa in the living room, where we could sit and look out the window to watch the show. And it was going to be a show. Dad always plays dirty, and Ian plays dirtier to keep up with him. Fouling, and by that I mean pushing and shoving, started after a few honeymoon minutes of pure basketball. And there was trash talk, in sign language along with quite a bit of shouting, so we could keep up with all of it. A couple of times my mother asked me to translate what Ian was saying.

"He's saying Grandma could play better than Dad can," I said, with a snicker. "It's going to get ugly."

After a half hour, Mom got bored and went off to do her own stuff. I got a book and spread out on the couch. Dad and Ian stayed out there, their clothes wet with sweat, faces red, running back and forth at each other. I could hear them grunting and yelling, and while our neighbors probably wondered why they played when it seemed to make them so upset with each other, I knew it was what Dad wanted, and just what Ian needed. Before they started playing like that, Ian would get upset and lock himself in his room for hours. He wouldn't talk to anybody: he would hardly eat. It only got worse after Grandma died. And then Dad started challenging him to these games. He wanted Ian to let his anger out. He wanted him to leave it out on the court, to play it out against him, to do anything but keep it to himself. I glanced out the window and saw Ian tell Dad he was bored playing such an old man, and I knew it was working.

Two hours later, Ian and Dad limped into the house. They stank. Ian was bleeding from cuts on his elbow and both knees, and Dad had a giant bruise on his forehead and a long scrape down his hand. They were about to go into the living room, presumably to collapse, when my mother ran downstairs.

"Out!" she shouted, and I think she signed it too, but it's not really important, because it was very apparent that in no way was she going to let them sit on anything looking and smelling like that. She's never had all that much patience for the basketball games, saying something that gets you that close to an emergency room probably should be avoided, or at least toned down.

"Go shower now," she said crisply, and they each grabbed a bottle of water and quietly headed off to a different bathroom. After their showers, they went to their bedrooms, closed their doors, and we didn't hear from them again until dinner. That's how it always was. The game created a volcano, and then there was a cooling off period, and then afterwards, it was always better somehow. I wasn't sure how much better it could be this time, though. This was not a problem anyone could easily fix.

The letter had set our family off course, and it was eight-thirty before I realized I was starving. Mom ordered pizza for dinner, and when the doorbell rang, I paid for the pies while she got Ian and my father. They came downstairs slowly, a little hunched over, but I could tell that the game had given Ian some energy back. He had a subtle smirk on his face when he turned to Dad on the stairs and asked him if he needed any help getting to the table. Dad straightened up and told Ian he'd better work harder if he ever had hopes of beating him. I smiled to myself as I watched the next segment begin, the retelling of the basketball game, in between bites of pizza, where the only goal was to glorify oneself and point out the other's inadequacies. Mom and I could just as well have left them and gone out to the movies. Ian and Dad went on and on, and at one point Mom rolled her eyes at me, but I knew she was as relieved as I was.

11

After dinner, there was more texting and then Ian went into his room. He left the door open, and I saw him on his bed, reading. An open door is an open door, so I walked in.

"What's going on?" I asked him.

"What do you mean?" he said, too innocently. Ian can try to fake stuff with me, but that doesn't mean it will always work.

I expertly raised one eyebrow. *"The videophone? You're not using it because you don't want us to see what you're saying."*

Ian looked at me long and hard, then stood up and walked behind me, closing the door. He went back and sat down on the bed.

"Promise you won't tell."

I nodded.

"No. Promise. This is serious." And Ian looked very serious as he stared at me.

"Okay, okay. I promise. What is it?"

Ian let out a breath of air. *"We're not going to accept this decision without doing something about it. We have to show them what this means to us."* Ian paused. He seemed to be considering whether to go on. When he did, his signs were deliberate and clear.

"We're going to take over a building at school. We're going to have a sit-in, and stay there until they change the decision to close Hawthorne."

I stared back at Ian for a long while, my hands on my hips. A sit-in. I couldn't think of anything to say, so I asked the most practical question that came to mind.

"What building?"

"Veditz, you know it. It's the building with the auditorium. There are offices upstairs, and a small kitchen. It's big, so if a lot of people come, we'll have enough space."

I felt like a little kid, blinking my eyes too many times, trying to make sense of Ian's plan. *"That building is in the middle of everything."*

Ian nodded. *"Exactly. You need to pick a place that is in the middle of things. We got the idea in history class with Mr. Kennelly."* He fingerspelled the word *civil disobedience.*

"It's a way to disagree, to show everyone how important Hawthorne is to us."

"Is Mr. Kennelly going to be there too?" I asked.

"Of course not. Students only. The teachers don't know anything about it."

The idea, the whole plan, was sinking in. *"How long will you be there?"*

Ian smiled. *"We're prepared to sleep there, in sleeping bags. Like a big slumber party."*

"But how long do you think that will be?"

Ian shrugged. *"As long as it takes,"* he signed calmly, and then paused. *"I don't care how long it takes."*

Ian's words tumbled around in my head. I realized I was starting to feel something that was different than anything I'd felt before. In fact, it was the opposite of the way I usually felt. I was used to feeling shy. I was used to being unsure about whether to answer a question in class, only to have someone else answer it instead. I was used to feeling too awkward to get up and dance.

But the way I felt, suddenly, out of nowhere, was new, and it felt good. I kept looking at Ian, and my hands started moving. In that moment, I knew that what I was saying was the most important thing I had ever said to my brother.

"I'm coming with you."

Ian smiled. *"Thanks, but that's okay. We'll handle it."*

My eyes locked on Ian's as I answered him. *"I'm sure you'll handle it, but I'm still coming with you."*

Ian shrugged his shoulders. *"You can't come. Mom and Dad won't let you."*

I rolled my eyes at him. *"And you were planning on asking them for permission?"* I asked sarcastically.

"No." Ian stopped smiling, and looked at me carefully. I knew what he was thinking; I could imagine the thoughts flying through his mind. He could see that I was serious. He also knew that Lisa had been gone just a few weeks, and I knew he and my parents often worried about me. Was I strong enough? And what would Mario say if he showed up with his hearing sister?

Ian looked apprehensive; he was rubbing his hands together distractedly. I knew I could have shrugged and told him to forget it, right then, and Ian would have appreciated my offer, but I had no intention of doing that. I had no idea if I did have the energy to join him. *Was* I strong enough? The facts didn't look too good. I still woke up most nights with nightmares. I could cry at the drop of a hat. I had a perpetual stomach ache which got worse every time I thought of anything having to do with Lisa. And yet, somehow there was a part of me that felt that despite all of those facts, or maybe because of them, I could do this. I could do something for Ian. I finally knew what it felt like to realize what you wanted to do, and know you would do it. I was going to Hawthorne. And I guess he understood that too, because he nodded slightly, looked me in the eye, and mouthed, *okay*.

I smiled, and sat down on Ian's bed. He described the plan, which he and his friends had plotted for over a month, and told me what had to be done next. He was in charge of food, and we would need to get to the supermarket and buy as much of it as we could. Nya had asked her parents if she could borrow the car Monday morning in order to bring props to school for a play. He would use the same excuse for why he would miss the bus, and get a ride to school instead. We would need to hide the food until Nya arrived to pick Ian up after my parents left for work.

Ian got up and paced back and forth in his room. *"What about you? How will you get out of going to school?"*

I looked out the window at a squirrel gnawing at an acorn on the sill. *"Mom and Dad leave for work before I go to school. I just need to look like I'm getting ready."*

Ian nodded. *"We can't get caught. You'll have to be very careful. Okay?"*

"I know," I said. There was one question I had to ask. *"Are you going to tell Nya and Mario I'm coming?"*

He kept pacing, but he slowed down a bit. He picked up a basketball and shook his head no. Ian tossed the basketball from one hand to the other, and walked, deep in thought. I didn't ask anymore. I knew Ian wasn't sure what Mario would think about me showing up. Mario liked me; it wasn't about that, it was deeper than that. I was an outsider, even though I was Ian's sister, even though I could sign. Ian was choosing to take a chance and bring me along, rather than have to win an argument with Mario first.

On Sunday morning my parents went out to brunch, inviting us along, but Ian glanced at me quickly and said we were going to stay behind and finish up some homework. This should have been my parents' first clue that something was up, but they were still too much in happy-she's-not-lying-in-her-bed and glad-he's-not-breaking-glass-objects mode to notice that homework was the last thing on our minds. Ian smiled his sweet, innocent smile and asked if we could use the car to go get some ice cream, if we finished our work. That's how we got the keys, the car, and a few hours all to ourselves.

As soon as they were gone, Ian ran up to his room and pulled a large manila envelope out of his drawer. When I asked him what it was, he opened it and I peeked inside. It was stuffed with cash.

"Excuse me? What is all that?" I asked him.

"That's what we're using for the food. Everyone pitched in. There's three or four weeks of allowance and candy money in here," Ian told me, and patted the packet.

"How much is there?"

"Two hundred dollars," Ian answered confidently.

"Two hundred?" I was shocked. It seemed like a lot of money. *"Do you really need that much?"*

Ian nodded his head vigorously at me. *"Of course, you'll see. We have to get food for everyone. I don't know if this is going to be enough."*

We got into the car and Ian drove us to the supermarket. We each got a cart and started slowly walking the aisles. Ian didn't have a list, but he seemed to know exactly what he wanted. Some of the kids had scoped out Veditz the week before, and Ian knew the small kitchen had a small oven. We would be able to boil water. Ian cleaned out a shelf of ramen noodles and tossed them into our carts. We added three jars of peanut butter and just as much jelly. We stared at the bread aisle for a long time, wondering how many loaves we would need. Ian settled on five. While he got pasta, I counted out two dozen apples. We dropped bags of pretzels and a bunch of chocolate bars into the carts. They were filling up fast, but it didn't seem like we had anything close to enough.

We walked by the "dental" aisle, and I would have kept walking, but Ian stopped and motioned to the shelf.

"We should probably get a few of these," he said. *"Some people are probably going to forget to bring theirs."*

I looked at him. Somehow, discussing whether or not we needed to throw toothbrushes and toothpaste into the carts had solidified the idea in my mind that we were talking about more than just one night. *"Ian, how long are we going to be there?"*

"I told you, as long as it takes. I don't know." He paused, and we looked each other in the eye. This was serious business. He didn't know. Ian nodded over to the shelf. *"So, should I get some?"*

"I guess so," I answered, and Ian tossed a bunch of toothbrushes and two tubes of toothpaste into the cart. It seemed like a good idea, but our budget was taking a hit. Ian stopped to look over what we already had, and consider how much it was costing us. I stood next to him, hands on my hips, as he rifled through the items in the carts.

"Hey," someone said behind me, and I turned around quickly, twisting my neck. It was a voice I knew, and hearing it sent a tingle down my spine.

"Ow, ow," I said as I massaged the back of my neck, looking up at Sandoval.

"Sorry, I didn't mean to startle you like that," he said. "You okay?"

"Oh yeah, I'm fine." The pain started to fade as I realized that Sandoval was about to meet my brother.

I looked over at Ian, who had a small smirk on his face. He was leaning his elbows on his cart, eyebrows floating up on his forehead, waiting for me to introduce him.

"Ian," I said and signed at the same time, "this is my friend Sandoval." I fingerspelled Sandoval's name as Ian stood up and stuck his hand out. Sandoval shook it, in a weird 1950's ritual that was freaking me out. Sandoval shuffled his feet shyly and his eyes looked even more amazing than usual, and that was freaking me out too. Ian nodded and signed *nice to meet you.* I interpreted. Sandoval didn't know where to look when he said, "Yeah, you too."

Ian smiled and told me he was going to get another cart, because he thought we would have enough money for more stuff. When he'd gone, I looked over at Sandoval. I could not think of a thing to say. After weeks of hanging out, what in the world had suddenly made this so awkward? Was it that he had walked into our secret mission? Or was it that the minute I heard his voice, I suddenly felt the way I had when Lisa and I spent hours whispering about him. I noticed him eyeing our carts and our very strange collection of food.

"So that's your brother," he said. "I never met someone who was deaf-mute before."

I winced.

"Don't say that. We don't say that," I said quickly, and then stopped myself. We? Was I part of a "we"?

"Don't say what?" Sandoval asked, looking as if I'd just told him he'd said something wrong. Which, in fact, was exactly what I'd done.

"Deaf-mute. Ian is Deaf. He doesn't hear."

"But he doesn't talk. Isn't that mute?" he asked, as if it were obvious.

"Ian isn't mute because there's nothing wrong with his voice. He just never heard people talking, so it's really hard to know how to make those sounds. Speaking is a skill, and he can do it, if he wants to or needs to, but it's not the way he communicates. It's not a 100% thing for him, like signing is." I took a breath, and realized I'd been talking very fast. "Does that make sense?" I asked quietly.

Sandoval stared at me like he was seeing something for the first time.

"Yeah, it does, I think. I never thought about it before." Sandoval stuck his hands in his pockets and rocked on his heels. We were both searching for something to say, I could feel it. Sandoval looked from me to our carts. He'd found what he was looking for. "Are you going on a camping trip?" he asked.

"Ummm," I stalled and shuffled my feet. "Yeah, something like that." At that moment, I wanted to tell him, not just to explain what we were doing with all that food, but to say something to take the weirdness away. But my quick mental calculations told me I couldn't take that risk. It wasn't my secret to tell.

I heard another cart squeaking down the aisle and knew Ian was back before I saw him. "So I'll see you," I said, starting to move my cart.

"Yeah, see you at lunch," Sandoval answered, which made it that much worse. I wasn't going to be at lunch. I'd be more than a hundred miles away. He would find out eventually, probably in Social Studies, but it mattered that he'd start out thinking I hadn't shown up. It mattered a lot.

Ian waved at Sandoval and he waved back as he moved away from us down the aisle, disappearing around the corner. Ian didn't say anything at first. We struggled to push three carts down the next aisle, adding items as we went. In front of the cookie aisle, he leaned his elbows on one of the carts again.

"So that's Mr. You-Know-Who?" he asked with one hand. I nodded. I didn't want him to be, but he was.

12

It seemed wrong to leave and not say anything, but at the same time, what do you say? *Mom and Dad, don't wait up, we've gone to take over a building.*

Probably not.

We waited for my parents to go to work, then left a note. We kept it simple, short and sweet.

Mom and Dad,
I need to do something about what is happening to Hawthorne. Shelly came with me. Don't worry — we'll be fine.
Love, Ian

A half hour later Nya pulled up in front of our house in a red station wagon. I looked out my window as Ian stepped out of the house and walked down the stairs. They hugged, the way everyone Ian knew greeted each other. A hug hello, a hug goodbye; it was just what everyone seemed to do when they hadn't seen each other in a while. They talked for a few minutes and then walked back into the house. I picked up my sleeping bag and backpack and went downstairs. Nya looked up at me and smiled.

"*Hi,*" she gestured, and I waved back. Ian pointed to all our bags of groceries, and we started carrying them out to the car. We threw in the sleeping bags, pillows and some blankets Ian found in the basement. Ian shoved our bags in, and then went back to check the house. He came back and signed, *"I almost forgot to call my dorm counselor to say I'd be late."* He shook his head, frustrated with himself. *"We're ready. Let's go."*

Nya got into the driver's seat, and Ian opened the car door and got in on the passenger side. I pulled on the rear door handle. It was locked. I knocked on the window, realizing at the same time that of course they couldn't hear me. Ian glanced back and saw I couldn't get in. He reached over and unlocked the door. I slipped into the back seat and slammed the door in time to see Nya do a double-take and raise her eyebrows at Ian. He looked back at her and didn't make a move.

"You already told Mario?" she asked. I expected her to ask that question. After all, I'd asked it myself. But it annoyed me a bit this time. I didn't like feeling like I was an intruder. It wasn't a nice feeling.

Ian shook his head no, moving only slightly.

Nya nodded and signed, *"This is going to be fun,"* in that sarcastic, exaggerated sort of way someone does when they don't expect something to be fun at all. We all knew Mario; he would say whatever he thought when he saw me, no doubt about that. Nya sighed, and then turned back and smiled at me. Then she turned the key in the ignition, and we were on our way to Hawthorne.

Ian and Nya chatted about the plans for how the sit-in would start. I tried to keep up, but it's harder to follow a signed conversation from the back seat of a car. I wasn't quite sure how Nya managed to drive and keep up with the conversation at the same time, but she seemed to be able to do it without much effort. Twenty minutes into the ride, I fell asleep with my head against the window.

I woke up as the car pulled into a parking spot behind Veditz Hall on the Hawthorne campus. It took a moment to remember where I was, and why. I needed to go to the bathroom. As soon as we got out of the car, Ian sent a text message to someone. Moments later, three other friends appeared, and after a quick round of greetings, began removing the groceries, sleeping bags and other supplies we'd brought. They moved swiftly and quietly, trying not to attract any attention. During the week Veditz was hardly used, except for auditorium events, and Mario had already scoped out an empty room in which to hide all the stuff. Just as the last of the stash was cleared out of the trunk, I looked up to see Mario walking towards us.

"What's up?" Ian asked him.

"They got the message that you and Nya were coming in late. What took you so long to call them?"

Ian used a sign that basically meant the thought had slipped his mind. I like that sign. Like so many in American Sign Language, it perfectly captured the idea -- a finger slipped down from between two fingers of the other hand. The thought dropped out of his head, gone.

"They almost called your parents," Mario said, already agitated. His cheeks were red and I could tell he had been pulling at his wild blond hair. It stood out from his head like waves of wheat. And he hadn't even seen me yet.

"Did they call my parents?" Ian asked aggressively, and stepped towards him. Mario shook his head no. *"And what if they did? I told them I was driving up with Nya."*

"To bring props for a play that doesn't exist. They would have gotten suspicious."

"So? They're going to find out soon enough. Anyway, it's over. Nothing happened."

Mario took a breath and I could see his body relax. Ian had a way with Mario. His temper didn't bother him, but Ian never backed down either. Somehow, it tended to allow Mario to stop, and think. Mario straightened his hair with his hands and looked over at Nya, who, at that moment, happened to be looking at me. He did his own double-take, his eyes opening wide. Mario shifted his body, hands on his hips, and stared at me.

Maybe it just seemed that way, but everyone around us froze, waiting to see what Mario would do. I was waiting too, so aware of the sudden abundance of quiet. The morning had turned hot and some kind of insect was buzzing around my ear, but I didn't move to swat it away. I straightened my back as I watched Mario's face for his reaction, readying myself for what was coming.

But as I looked back at him, I could see that he wasn't angry, or even surprised. He studied me, as if I were a puzzle he was figuring out, and then he took a deep breath. He slowly walked towards me, and even though I was barely twenty paces away, it felt like we were in a movie filmed in slow motion. When Mario reached me, he held his arms open, and caught me in a hug that was strong and gentle at the same time.

Something about the way he held me, my head against his chest, one hand on my hair, reminded me that it was the first time I'd seen him since Lisa died, since Ian had left his house in the middle of the night. And suddenly I felt ashamed. I was many things to Mario, not just a cardboard cut-out of The Hearing Sister of his best friend. If I hadn't realized it before, I knew it now. Ian had banked on it, and he'd been right.

Mario held onto me for a few moments, and when he let go, he rubbed my head like you do with a puppy. Mario and

I were okay. And a nod from Mario meant everyone else would give me a chance, too. More importantly though, I was where I wanted to be. I felt it in my stomach, the same way I'd felt it that day in Ian's room when I'd first heard about the plan. No matter what happened, I knew that I had done the right thing.

Mario's hug had said everything he needed to say, and so when he moved away, he went right into action mode, checking his watch and listing everything that needed to happen next. At eleven-thirty, fifteen minutes away, everyone who was taking part in the sit-in would gather at Veditz. Even if they were in a class, which most of them would be, they were supposed to stand up and quietly leave. Mario checked on the supplies, and then, we waited.

Hawthorne is a large campus with old stone buildings and open lawns. At eleven-thirty, our small group sat on the steps leading to Veditz and watched as students slowly approached. At first there were just a few, walking towards us on the lush grass, but within minutes, we could see kids coming at us from every corner of the campus. The sight was almost overwhelming. We stood up as the first of them reached us, and Mario ushered them into the building, slapping hands or bumping fists or hugging each and every one. The call had gone out to every middle school and high school member, and it looked to me like everyone was showing up to take part.

A girl with long hair walked by me and smiled at Ian in a way that let me know it was Alexia even before he told me himself. He quickly fingerspelled her name at his side after she'd passed, as if sharing a secret. He had told me they'd been talking to each other more, and spending some time together after class, but not much more than that.

"What do you mean, not much more than that?" I'd teased, when the subject of Alexia came up a few days before.

Ian had rolled his eyes, his cheeks flushing. *"I'm not telling you anything anymore if you're going to be like that."*

I'd smiled and poked him, delighted that there was finally something in the world that could turn my brother into mush. And even though he said he wouldn't talk about her, he did, asking questions about what I thought she meant by this or that, and what I thought he might do next. Ian was asking my opinion, a person who had not yet been on a date, but who nevertheless was an expert simply because we were both girls, and as Ian said, *similar.*

"Similar, how?"

Ian shrugged. *"Sensitive. Quiet."*

I pretended to yawn.

"No!" He'd laughed. *"Not boring at all! I can't stop thinking about her!"*

And here she was, looking like she might be spending time thinking about Ian, too.

Mario continued to usher students into the building, instructing everyone to move quickly. Over a hill, we spotted some teachers approaching.

"Hurry up! Get inside. We need to close the doors!"

Students streamed in, backpacks in hand. More supplies, no doubt, packed in each of them. Suddenly, Mario eyed someone in the crowd. He motioned to little Ciara to come out, and she and three of her friends stepped closer to Mario.

"What are you doing here?" he asked her. *"You can't go in there!"*

The teachers were coming closer now, waving their hands to get our attention. Everyone ignored them.

Ciara's face was set in what could only be described as a mean stare. *"Why not?"* she asked. *"Why can't we be part of the sit-in?"*

Mario glanced over his shoulder at the teachers, some gesturing, some shouting, now only a few yards away.

"Because you're too young. They won't allow little kids to stay here."

Ciara gave Mario an incredulous look. *"Who? Them, or you? This is my school, too. You'll be gone soon, but I won't have anywhere to go!"*

Mario looked stunned. He glanced over to Nya, and then Ian. They nodded quickly. We all ran into the hall, and bolted the door just as the teachers reached the steps. Mario looked over at Ciara. *"Be good,"* he warned. *"Don't make me regret this."*

There was pounding at the door, which I could hear but Mario could feel. He turned to the crowd of students behind us. There were almost forty all together. This might not seem like much, but in a shrinking school, it was a lot. It was everyone.

"Let's go upstairs." Mario stood up on a chair and signed in a broad, exaggerated way so that everyone in the crowd could see. *"Nya and Ian and I will go out onto the balcony and explain what's happening. Settle down; we're going to be here for a while! Remember, don't disturb anything; do not break anything. We want to make a point, to show them what we are willing to do to save our school. That's what we're going to tell them. I'll come and talk to all of you soon."*

Upstairs, above the auditorium, there was a large, empty room, with a balcony attached that overlooked the front lawn of the school. There was a small kitchen off the room as well. This was where Ian, Nya and Mario planned for everyone to sleep, eat and stay for the length of the sit-in.

One giant slumber party. We filed into the room, and slowly sat down on the floor.

With Ian headed towards the balcony, I found myself suddenly alone, and felt a momentary pang of panic. I recognized some of Ian's friends in the crowd, and a few of the kids who were always in his plays. A couple of students were looking at me and signing quietly to each other. Whispering. I knew, of course, what they were saying. *Who is she? His sister? What is she doing here?*

Just then, someone tapped me on the shoulder. I looked over at Alexia, who smiled down at me. Seeing her was a relief. I didn't really know her, but at that moment she was the friendliest face in the room.

"Hi, *A-L-E-X-I-A*," I fingerspelled.

"*You know who I am?*" she said, surprised.

Caught, I tried to think fast to cover up my mistake, and found that I couldn't. "*Ian has told me a lot about you,*" I answered honestly. "*He pointed you out to me when you came in.*"

Alexia smiled again, and I thought her cheeks reddened a bit.

"*Can I sit with you?*"

It was my turn to smile, and I nodded as she settled herself down on the floor next to me. Outside, I could see Mario engaging in a long conversation with someone below him. By now, the principals of the middle and high schools and superintendent had likely been alerted, and if they weren't there on the lawn, they were certainly on their way. Ian had worried that the sit-in would cause trouble for these people, who were not to blame for the decision to close. "*It's completely at the state level, the governor and state assembly,*" he'd explained. "*The administrators have no more power than we do.*"

"*It'll be obvious that they didn't have anything to do with it,*" I'd said. "*How will they be to blame?*"

"We won't leave when they tell us to," he signed quietly and then shrugged. *"But we have no choice."*

Alexia took a bag of red licorice out of her backpack and offered me some. I thanked her and bit into the chewy candy. Alexia's backpack was stuffed; she had to pull the sides together to get the zipper closed again. Her curly brown hair fell in front of her eyes as she struggled with the bag, and I reached over to help her. Together, we got the bag closed, but not before I caught a peek at the treasure Alexia had brought with her. She had the equivalent of a small candy store stuffed inside.

"You really like candy," I said.

Alexia smiled but looked embarrassed. *"I knew everyone else would bring the real food, so I thought I'd make sure to bring something sweet."*

I smiled back at her. *"Just tell me I can sit with you for as long as we're here,"* I signed. Alexia laughed, her blue eyes shining like glass.

Ian stepped back into the room and raised his hand for everyone to look towards him.

"We talked to the principal. Mr. Sinclair isn't happy. That's not really a surprise. As soon as he can figure out who is in here, our parents will be called. He says he is concerned for our safety. He will call the police to come in, but we expected that."

"Police?" Deyquan stood up, and everyone looked his way. He was a friend of Ian's, and Nya's boyfriend. *"Why would they call the police?"*

"To keep other kids from coming in. No one will be allowed back into the building if they leave. They think we're copying Gallaudet, so they're worried."

I knew about Gallaudet, the university for Deaf students in Washington D.C. Students there held two major protests, almost twenty years apart, to fight for their rights and get the college president they wanted. The protests each lasted many days. Both times, the students won.

Ian looked towards the balcony where Nya was motioning. It was hard to see her, but Ian seemed to understand what she was signing. She seemed to be asking him a question, and he paused a moment and then nodded, signing *agreed*.

He turned back to the crowd. *"The superintendent has asked us to unbolt the door, in case there is any kind of emergency and we have to leave quickly. They will not enter unless we allow them to. We agreed to this request."*

Ian crossed his arms in front of his chest and scanned the room. He glanced in my direction and saw me and Alexia sitting together, and a small smile appeared on his lips. He put his arms down and continued.

"If anyone wants to leave, at any time, please feel free to leave. No one will be angry or disappointed. Coming today showed how unified we are, but this will not be easy. It probably feels fine now, but this floor looks pretty hard…"

A laugh went up around the room. Ian smiled. *"Really, we appreciate it if someone stays for fifteen minutes, or…"* He held up his hands. *"We don't know how long this will last, so we need to take care of ourselves while we're here. Soon we'll break up into teams for our food - breakfast, lunch and dinner. Everyone will sleep in this room, so feel free to spread out and get comfortable."*

"And…" Mario stepped forward and turned towards Ciara and her friends in the corner of the room. *"Watch out for the little ones, too."*

Ciara rolled her eyes. *"We'll see who's here last, Mario,"* she signed.

Mario's eyebrows raised two inches as he laughed. *"You're challenging me? Okay little girl, we'll see who's still here when it's all over."* With that, he walked over to Ciara and they linked pinkies for the dare. He was still laughing as he walked away. *"The babies are taking over,"* he signed to Nya as he chuckled.

Alexia got up and spread her sleeping bag out on the floor. She propped her pillow up against the wall and sat down again, making herself comfortable, as Ian had instructed. She handed me some more licorice.

"I forgot," I signed as I ate. *"You moved here from where?"*

"California. North of San Francisco. I haven't been here very long."

I told her our family had taken a trip to San Francisco several years before, and we talked about her favorite places. After that, we moved on to school and what we liked and didn't like. In addition to her stash of sweets, Alexia was easy to talk to; I could see why Ian liked her. She had a quick smile and asked good questions, questions that made me think and kept us talking for an hour before I'd realized how much time had passed. All around us, kids were chatting, telling stories. The scene was anything but quiet. I smiled, and Alexia asked me what was funny.

"I was just thinking that hearing people are always saying that Deaf people live in a silent world, but if they spent five minutes in here, they'd really be surprised."

"I know, my grandparents said the same thing. They said they used to think that way, and then they had my dad, and they said it opened up a new world."

"Your dad's deaf?" I asked, even though I was pretty sure that that was what she'd just said.

She nodded. *"And my mom, and me, and my brother."*

"Wow," I said, and then I let that information bounce around in my head for a while. What a difference, I thought, between Alexia and Ian. Alexia grew up in a family where, from the day she was born, everyone knew how to

communicate with her. They knew, because it simply was what they did. It had been so different for Ian.

My parents often told the story of how Ian was born before hospitals screened babies for deafness, and that they'd needed to fight with his doctor to have his hearing tested. He was bright-eyed and curious, so when he didn't say any words at one, or one-and-a-half, his doctor said to give him time. At two, he said the same thing, even though my mother says she told him she knew something was different about Ian. He didn't startle like other toddlers he played with on the playground. At the same time, he was alert and communicated by pointing and pulling her places. The doctor called her an overprotective first-time mother. Maybe he did just need time.

"I was a nurse, for goodness sakes," my mother always says when she talks about it all. "I was a nurse and I couldn't see that my baby couldn't hear a thing."

One day she was washing a glass bowl when it slipped from her hands and smashed into a million pieces on the floor. Ian didn't look up from the cars he was playing with, his back to the shattered glass lying around my mother.

After that, his doctor agreed to the hearing test, but my mother already knew the results. When Ian was two-and-a-half, our parents received the diagnosis. Ian was profoundly deaf. When they weren't working, Mom and Dad traveled to different specialists and schools to try and figure out what to do for him. They settled on sign language, but that wasn't an end in any way, only a beginning.

Once, a college friend of my mother's visited and I overheard her telling the story. My mother's voice had become quiet and strained, and I'd looked up from doing my homework in the kitchen. I was in fifth or sixth grade. Her words stayed with me, I guess, because it was the first time I could remember hearing my mother sound so sad.

"So we decided on sign language, which I don't regret, of course. But he's two-and-a-half, and then three, and a therapist is coming to the house to teach him, and he's picking it all up so fast. And at first, so am I, but then he started going to a special preschool, and suddenly, I couldn't keep up. And I still can't. There are times when I have no idea what he's saying, and I have to ask my own son to repeat himself. Do you know how terrible that feels?"

The friend said, "Maybe you shouldn't have chosen sign language. Some kids learn to speak."

I remember my mother sighing the way people do when they know they're talking to someone who hasn't got a clue. "Sign language is his natural language, his native language. Speaking is a skill he's learning in school as well. We adapt to each other." Her voice had changed. She was no longer sharing feelings but relaying facts, educating, informing. "If you could see him sign," she'd said, "you would understand."

Mario laughed out loud across the room, and I startled, realizing I'd been sitting with a piece of licorice in my hand, staring off into space. I would have worried that Alexia thought I was strange, but she'd pulled a cell phone out of a pouch in her backpack and was reading a text message.

"My mom," she signed. *"Looks like school is calling our parents."*

Just then Ian walked over. He smiled at us both, and handed me his cell phone. I looked at the message typed on the small screen.

IS SHE OK?

"Who?" I asked.

"Dad."

"Is that all he said?"

Ian nodded. He took back the phone, and typed in, SHE'S FINE. DON'T WORRY. Ian sat down next to me and we waited for my father to type back. He didn't.

"Seems like school sent out an email, and then started calling everyone," Alexia signed with one hand, texting with the other.

"Doesn't look like Dad is too happy about it," Ian said. Neither of us said a thing for a few minutes. A picture of our father, angry, was easy to imagine. In all the planning we'd done for the sit-in, we hadn't spent any time at all thinking about the reaction our family would have, along with the impact, the consequences. Now that we'd gotten a first look at my father's response, there wasn't a whole lot to say. Hopefully he'd understand, and Mom, too. And if not, there wasn't much we could do about it.

Ian stood up and clapped his hands together, and I knew this was his way of saying, 'moving on.' He got everyone's attention by waving his arms and stamping his foot a few times. He explained the way we'd prepare meals, in teams, and then a spirited discussion ensued on how everyone would split up into teams. I made it onto the breakfast team with Alexia, which was just fine with me. As far as I knew, breakfast would look a lot like cereal, and that was something I could handle. Ian got a group of people together and they went off to the kitchen, to organize the supplies everyone brought.

I scanned the room. Everywhere there was motion, conversations starting and stopping all around me. Most of the people in the room signed without using their voices, but sounds were still part of the way some communicated. Some people signed and spoke at the same time. Some had cochlear implants, devices surgically implanted that enabled them to perceive sound. Some of the students were profoundly deaf; some were hard of hearing. Once at our house I'd seen Mario use a hearing aid so he could talk on the phone. But most of the time he signed, voice off, and with so much energy and passion that it was hard not to stare at him.

I spotted Mario nearby, only to notice him looking at me. He was chewing on his lip, as if he were considering whether or not to do something. Mario stopped chewing, and motioned for me to come near him. I got up and walked over.

"Shelly, do you think you could listen and tell us what they're saying?" He motioned with his head over to the balcony. I could hear people speaking on the lawn below.

I nodded. I felt a flutter of nerves, quickly wondering whether I could actually do what he was asking, but most of all, I was pleased. It felt good to be asked.

Mario explained how he wanted me to sit, my back against the balcony bars, facing away from the crowd, so that he could "listen in" without anyone knowing it.

"You've got a real mess on your hands here." I signed the words of the police officer. He was talking to the superintendent, Mr. Giancola, just a few feet away from the balcony.

I tried to copy the interpreters I'd seen over the years at school. I identified the speakers, and then shifted my body to represent each one as they spoke.

"What do you suggest we do?"

"This is what you do. You wait. In situations like these, you never go in by force. You'll have a riot on your hands. You've got to just wait them out."

"But there are some little kids in there. Four nine-year-olds. Who knows how long the others intend to stay. I can't let the younger ones be there overnight." The superintendent sounded worried, and I tried to show how he sounded on my face.

"Look, that might be, but all you can do is ask them to come out. Get their parents over here. But I've been watching the older ones, just like you. They're not going to give up so easily."

Mario watched me intently, and now Deyquan and Nya were looking on as well. Ian appeared in the doorway and seemed startled at first to see me, sitting on the floor of the balcony signing dramatically, to match the drama below. Signing the opposite of the way I usually signed, but it wasn't me talking. Ian looked over at Mario and glared at him. Why?

The superintendent cleared his throat. "So you're suggesting we allow them to sleep there?"

"I don't see any other way. It's only four o'clock; some of them might give up and leave, but I'm betting most will stay. We'll keep officers here all night, to keep an eye on things. Tell me, though, what is it that they want?"

The superintendent didn't say anything for a moment. I waited, listening carefully. Mario made a small motion that meant 'what?' and I shrugged slightly.

"They want to save this school," Mr. Giancola said, clearing his throat again. "I don't think they will, but I don't blame them for trying." He let out a low chuckle, and I was surprised to hear him laugh. "In fact, I'd rather be in there with them than out here right now."

There was silence again and I glanced down between the balcony bars. Mr. Giancola extended his hand and shook the police officer's. Then he walked away to talk to a group of officers nearby. I looked up at Mario. He was smiling.

"I wondered what he thought of all this." He motioned for me to follow him back inside the room, and then turned towards me. *"Thank you Shelly. You did a great job. Maybe someday you'll be an interpreter?"*

I smiled back at him, and shrugged my shoulders again. Me, an interpreter?

I felt a hand grab hold of my arm and looked over to see Ian, his face angry and red. *"That's enough."*

"Hey," Mario's hands gestured 'Calm down' the way Ian had done to him many times before. *"She was just interpreting. She's good at it. What's the problem?"*

"She didn't come here to work," Ian signed tersely.

Now it was Mario's turn to play the Ian role, to be the calmer one. *"She wasn't working. She was just helping us out. That's why she came here."*

His words distracted me from what was going on in front of me. Ian's anger at seeing me interpret was confusing, but what Mario said confused me even more. Is that why I had come with Ian, to help? I liked helping, and I was pleased I'd done well, but I didn't think that that had been my reason for tagging along. The simple answer, of course, was that I'd wanted to show Ian that I cared about what was happening to him. Somehow though, I knew that that wasn't the whole story either. Why had I come?

"Forget it," Ian signed, interrupting my rambling thoughts, and he walked away from both of us.

I looked at Mario and he shrugged at me. *"It's nothing,"* he signed.

"It seems like something. He seems really mad." I didn't like it when Ian got like that, especially when it had anything to do with me.

"He's not mad, he's worried." And then Mario looked at me the way he had when he'd first seen me outside on the steps, and the world outside Hawthorne, the world in which I no longer had my best friend, rammed into this world, the world that belonged to my brother. I breathed in sharply, and then let the breath out.

"I'm okay," I said. I signed the words deliberately. It was the truth; I was okay. My heart was beating fast, my palms were a little bit sweaty, and the ever-present ache was there in my chest, but I was okay. And I had just done something completely scary and strange and, yes, exhilarating. Mario put his hand on my shoulder and smiled. Then a guy named Samir came over and asked for some help, and he was off.

I scanned the room for Ian, and found him sitting with Alexia on her sleeping bag. I hesitated, not wanting to get in their way, but Ian caught my eye and waved me over. I walked towards them slowly, and sat down at the edge of my sleeping bag.

"Sorry," Ian signed sheepishly.

I shrugged my shoulders. *"No problem,"* I answered. Ian nodded and smiled.

"I should go back out there and talk to Mr. Giancola. Calm him down," Ian said. *"See you later,"* he said to Alexia.

"See you later," she answered, smiling at Ian in a way that made me look away for a moment, it felt so personal.

13

After Ian had gone, I slipped back into my spot on my sleeping bag, sitting with my back against the wall. Alexia rummaged through her bag again, this time pulling out a small bottle of bright red nail polish. She kicked off her shoes, and shook the bottle.

"Do you like this color?" she asked.

I took off my sneakers and socks, and wiggled my toes, which seemed like just the right way to answer her. I smiled at Alexia. She was already done with one foot and halfway through the other. I watched her carefully paint her toenails, each one a glistening red. When she was done, she put the small brush back in the bottle and handed it to me. I started on one of my big toes while she looked at me.

"I talked to your brother about you," she said.

She'd taken me by surprise, and I didn't know what to say. *"What... um... what, what do you mean?"* I was used to tripping over my words in English, but here I was doing it in one-handed sign language.

"I saw what he did after Mario asked you to help him. He doesn't need to be that way. Hey, careful," Alexia said, and I quickly looked down to see the puddle of polish on the top of my nail, my hand frozen in place. I used it to paint

the other toes, thinking about what to say to Alexia at the same time.

"It's terrible, what happened to your friend," she continued. *"I'm really sorry."*

I took a breath, and put the brush back in the bottle. *"How do you know about that? Ian told you?"*

Alexia tilted her head back and forth as if to say yes, and no. *"He didn't say anything at first, but Mario knew. Ian came back after that weekend and didn't talk to anyone. He stayed in his room and wouldn't go to class. He just stayed in bed all day. He wouldn't even talk to Mario. Mario called your parents. The social worker came and talked with him, and then they left him alone."*

Alexia paused, and I looked down, taking it all in. I picked up the nail polish bottle and started in on my other foot, buying time to think. So Ian had reacted the same way I had, but he'd seemed so different when I saw him. He seemed so strong, but now I realized that he was strong for me. And that's what I needed him to be.

Still, finding out how he'd fallen apart at school made me see how hard it must have been for him, first to find out about Lisa, and then to take care of me.

"I'm sorry Shelly, I didn't mean to make you upset," Alexia said, her eyes wide. What did my face look like when I was thinking? She looked worried.

I shook my head. *"I'm not upset. I mean, well, I'm always upset, but not because of what you said right now."* I smiled at her. *"Actually it's really important for me to hear about that. I'm glad you told me."*

She didn't look convinced.

"Really," I signed. *"It's like... I was gone for a while, stuck inside my own head because everything hurt so much. I couldn't think of anything or anyone else. In the beginning it felt like I'd be like that forever, like I'd lost the connection to my life. The only person who could help me was Ian."*

I paused, and then continued. *"The thing I don't understand is: how did he do it? If he was so upset, how could he have been so strong for me?"*

Alexia smiled a small smile that showed in her eyes. *"I guess the same way that you're here now,"* she said, slowly and simply.

I leaned over, blowing on my toes and mulling over what she'd just said. I wiggled my new red toes, admiring the shiny color. They'd look good with my sandals.

I looked over at Alexia. *"I knew I had to come here. I knew it right away. And...I knew I could do it."*

She nodded, and in that moment, a thought hit me the way a baseball bat connects with a homerun ball. I had learned the word for it in English class when we read James Joyce. Epiphany. I was having an epiphany right there in Veditz Hall.

When Lisa died, I'd lost the footing I'd had in my life. But even before, I hadn't always felt solid. I spent so much time doubting myself. Lisa had been my cheerleader, my best friend, someone who really believed in me. It was impossible to believe that she was no longer alive. And even though I still didn't really believe it, I'd come to understand it. This was the way things were now. And I found myself waiting for a sign, waiting for a way to reconnect to my life. The funny thing was that the sign had come off my brother's fingers. *"We're taking over a building at school."* And somehow, in that moment, something in me changed, unlocked. I thought, "I'm going too," and I knew I would. I no longer had Lisa telling me all the things I could do; now the voice I heard was my own.

Alexia touched my shoulder and pointed to Ian, standing just inside the room near the balcony. He was motioning for me to come over, his eyes wide and his face tense.

"What's wrong? I asked from across the room, my heart starting to beat faster. *What's wrong?"*

His answer was simple. *"Mom and Dad."*

Mom and Dad? I didn't move, as this new development sunk in. This was something we hadn't planned for. We hadn't given any thought to it at all. Ian was ready to deal with Mr. Giancola and the principals. Our parents were another story.

I stood up and walked over to Ian, who was biting on his thumbnail.

"Stop that," I signed, surprisingly calm. *"Where are they?"*

Ian nodded his head towards the balcony, and we both stepped outside. He pointed to the left, and far off, I could make out our parents, walking towards the building. But they weren't just walking. My mother was lugging some kind of big box. My father struggled with something long and bulky that kept tipping to the left and right as he tried to balance it.

"What are they holding?" I said.

Ian shook his head. He didn't know. We'd have to wait and find out. Because they were loaded down with whatever it was they had with them, they walked so slowly it seemed to take forever for them to get close. As they approached the lawn in front of Veditz, I squinted and realized what they had with them.

"I think that's our tent," I signed, turning to Ian. *"Why do they have our tent?"*

He didn't answer. He was staring out over the lawn as if waiting for the answer to a question.

My father and mother were close now, close enough to stop and look up at us. Mom smiled and raised her hand in a small wave. She was dragging a large cooler behind her.

Dad didn't do anything. He didn't look mad, but he wasn't smiling either. We watched as he set the tent down on the ground. He looked up at Ian and they stared at each other for a few seconds. Then he turned back to the tent and started to set it up, right there on the lawn. We stared at him, stunned. Dad took a mallet out of the tent pack and started nailing stakes into the ground. Mr. Giancola began to approach him and then seemed to think better of it. He turned on his heel and walked over to one of the police officers, speaking quietly. As he and the officer spoke, our tent started to take shape.

Mom opened up the cooler and pulled out a white plastic bag. She handed it to my father. He turned to look at us, and then hurled the bag up to Ian. Ian caught it against his chest, which might have hurt a little, because I could hear it hit.

Ian balanced the bag in the crook of his arm and opened it. I peered inside at hundreds of jawbreakers, Ian's favorite candy. Enough jawbreakers, I guessed, for everyone. Good thing, I thought, that we'd brought all those toothbrushes.

Ian's face broke into a grin, matched by the look on Dad's face. Ian's body relaxed. He began to kid my dad about the sag on one side of the tent, but I knew that what he was really saying was thank you, thank you, thank you.

Our parents were first, but nowhere near the last. Ian watched as my mother explained how they'd used the emergency email alert to tell parents of their own plans to protest, and urge them to join in. Even as they were talking, people began streaming in, lugging more tents and equipment.

Slowly, it became clear that the lawn around Veditz was transforming into a colorful tent city, the kind we had seen in photographs of Gallaudet, but this time, filled with families instead of students. Mario's mother spread out a blanket on the ground while his father tied two ends of a sheet to a tree branch. In black marker he'd written: SAVE HAWTHORNE.

Not everyone, of course, had come to join in; Ciara's father angrily demanded she leave the building, threw around the words "sue" and "reckless" but with no result. He yelled at Mr. Giancola, at the police officers milling around, and finally, he yelled at Ciara when Mario brought her out to the balcony to see him. Ciara was unfazed; she leaned against the stone railing and told him, clearly and confidently, that she would be the last to leave.

"Like father, like daughter," I saw Mario say to Ian when Ciara came back in and plopped herself down on the floor with her friends. I couldn't help smiling. *"Like you,"* I thought. Her friends were beginning to look tired and a bit restless, but Ciara seemed the same as when she'd arrived six hours before – bright-eyed and raring for a fight.

Mario rallied us to get started on dinner, and I went to help. Deyquan, standing next to me, tapped me on the shoulder.

"Why are you here?" he asked abruptly. No "how's it going," no easing up to the big question. Just straight and to-the-point, which I'd come to recognize was part of Deaf culture. If your hair looked bad, you were going to hear about it. If someone wanted to know why you were the only hearing person at an all-Deaf sit-in, he'd just go ahead and ask.

What was the answer?

A bunch of possible replies flew through my head. I came to support Ian. I came to support Hawthorne. I came to help, to interpret. Maybe I came because I wanted to be a part of something important. Maybe I came because my best friend was dead.

Maybe I came because I wanted to, and because I could.

And then I knew the answer, the one that took all of those possibilities and rolled them into one.

"I came for me," I signed. And it was true.

Deyquan's serious face turned warm as he smiled. He couldn't possibly have understood the meaning behind what I said, but he knew I meant it. He was still studying me, but now it seemed more out of curiosity than suspicion.

"You could be outside with your parents. It will be more comfortable out there than in here later."

True, I thought, though Deyquan had obviously never slept in our tent.

I shrugged. *"I don't care. I want to be here."*

"If this is what you want..." he signed, raising his hands up to his shoulders, in a way that suddenly reminded me of my grandmother, because it was what she'd always do when we wanted something she couldn't quite understand. It made me giggle. Deyquan saw that and smiled even more.

"Too bad my sisters aren't here," he said in a wistful way.

I didn't answer, and we unpacked bags of fruit and potato chips in silence. At the bottom of one of the shopping bags, Deyquan found our stash of chocolate bars, and held up a fistful.

"Really?" he asked, looking at me. *"You guys forgot to buy tomato sauce but you remembered chocolate bars?"*

I made the sign for "mistake," giving him the oops-I-forgot-my-homework look I've been using since the third grade. Scrunched up nose, big eyes. Deyquan laughed.

"Whatever. Pasta with butter is good too. I found some in the refrigerator."

Even though I wasn't on dinner detail, I joined Deyquan as he filled Mario's enormous pot with water, and then placed it on the little stove. It took a long while for the water to boil, and while we waited, Deyquan asked me about our family and my school. He wanted to know who signed, and how well. He wanted to know if I thought Hawthorne would survive, and I told him I thought it would.

As we were talking, three of Ciara's little friends approached Mario. I could see them walking slowly closer to him, clearly afraid. One of the boys, a kid named Kaya, tapped Mario on the shoulder. As the chosen spokesperson, he explained that they were tired and hungry and thought maybe they should go back to the dorm. Mario nodded, and then shook each child's hand, thanking them for their contribution to the protest. You could see the kids relax, and stand up straighter. Then Mario brought them downstairs. Deyquan and I went out on the balcony and watched as the door below us opened, and Mario signaled to someone we couldn't see. It was getting dark. The parents out on the lawn approached the door to see what was going on. Mr. Giancola appeared, and ushered Kaya and his friends towards some adults, probably their parents. I saw him look back at Mario, and mouth the words "thank you."

By the time we got back, the water was at full boil, and we cooked as much pasta as we could fit into the pot. Samir helped us drain it once it was done, which wasn't easy without a strainer. Nya had plates and drinks ready, and some of the other kids had sliced apples and handed out granola bars. Deyquan dramatically put a pat of butter on each mound of spaghetti he plated, and we couldn't help laughing about it, even when the joke should have worn out long before.

After we'd eaten, Mario went out to talk to Mr. Giancola. I leaned into the doorway to see what was going on. He had Jacqueline, the interpreter, with him, and I could hear the tension in his voice. Many parents were gathered around him.

"Mario, you've made your point. It's time to stop."

Mario shook his head. *"Has someone from the state announced the decision to keep Hawthorne open? I haven't heard anything."*

"That's not going to happen and you know it. You can't stay in there overnight without adult supervision. Come out, and we'll find another way to protest the decision."

"This is our way. We're not leaving. The decision isn't fair, and no one is listening to us."

"Do you think this will make them listen to you?" Mr. Giancola's voice rose. Jacqueline signed his words but his own hands moved in dramatic gestures. "The decision is made, Mario. They made it a long time ago. They've kept the school open but don't give us any money to fix it. The place is falling apart."

Mr. Giancola ran his hands through his thinning hair. "You want to know how bad it is? You'd better hope it doesn't rain while you're in there. Veditz needed a new roof five years ago."

Mario repeated that we wouldn't leave, but I could see that something in his expression had changed. He seemed stunned, and I could understand why. If the decision really had been made long ago, could anything make a difference?

Mario came back into the hall, and Ian asked him what was up. Mario shook him off, and walked away. Ian looked at me.

"What happened?"

"Mr. Giancola said the school was falling apart." I left it at that. If Mario wanted to say more, he would. I had just been eavesdropping, anyway.

Ian and I walked out onto the balcony to talk to our parents. Every few hours we'd do that, to give them an update and show them we were doing okay. It was ten o'clock. My parents said they were going to sleep, and Mom asked for the hundredth time if we needed anything. *"Sweet dreams,"* Ian answered, and said we'd see them in the morning.

Not long after that, the storytelling began. It started with a funny story Deyquan told about the basketball team's trip to another residential school, and it went from there. The stories kept coming. Sitting on sleeping bags and snacking on the treats Alexia passed around made me feel like I was in a theater watching a live performance. Samir was hysterical. Two tenth grade girls, Miranda and Isabelle, mimicked their dorm counselors and left everyone laughing. Mario and Ian told old stories they'd seen passed down from teachers and other students. When I looked at my watch, it was 3 a.m.

14

My parents always said that the perfect sleepover would last exactly fourteen hours. They felt that after hour fourteen, the trouble started. Someone always cried. When I was a little kid I thought that was ridiculous, but I'd noticed that what they predicted often came true. It was certainly true at the sit-in.

We'd stayed up really late, and woken up early. We put breakfast together, but after that, there wasn't much else to do. The hours dragged on, and people got cranky. Samir and Deyquan got into an argument over what Ian should say to Mr. Giancola. Nya tried to be a peacemaker, but ended up fighting with Deyquan herself. By the time we were ready for lunch, they'd settled the argument, but it felt like at any moment, another one could break out.

Still, we weren't about to give up. Around noon, the arrival of local news crews helped bolster everyone's resolve. Ian made a chart, and every hour, someone would step out onto the balcony and talk eloquently about the school, and why it needed to stay open. It felt like poetry night all over again, and not just to me. When it was her turn, Ciara stepped onto a box so she could be seen over the railing, and signed the dandelion poem.

Mr. Giancola spoke to Mario, Nya, and Ian often, but the situation remained unchanged. He had nothing to report from the state, aside from the decision to maintain closure. He pleaded with everyone to leave. Many of the parents, who had seemed so supportive the day before, were getting tired. They were talking with Mr. Giancola too, and the news didn't sound good.

As the day turned into another night, we scraped together more meals and passed the time. There were only a few stories that night, and I could tell that more than a few people were starting to think the same thing: *how much longer?*

Just past two in the morning, it started to rain.

And exactly as Mr. Giancola had warned, it rained inside Veditz too. Deyquan and Nya scrambled to get waste paper baskets, and a kid named James grabbed our cooking pot and set it under a particularly bad spot to catch the dripping water. When James accidentally kicked a trash can over while trying to get back to his spot, Ciara's sleeping bag got soaked. Mario gave her his own instead. He stretched out on the floor with just his pillow under his head. It took almost an hour for everyone to get settled again, and by that time my head ached. I wished I'd brought something for it. I needed to sleep. All I wanted was to be in my own bed.

The next morning I heard rustling and I opened my eyes to see Alexia stepping over my sleeping bag to get closer to Ian. She tapped him gently on the shoulder until he woke up and looked at her.

"I can't stay," she said in small and quiet signs. *"I can't do this anymore. I'm so tired."*

I could tell she was crying. Ian reached up and smoothed her hair, which was a little wild and tangled. *"Don't worry, it's okay,"* he said. *"You should go home and go to sleep."*

Alexia nodded. And then she leaned over and kissed him.

I can't know for sure, but from the look of surprise on Ian's face, I guessed I'd just witnessed their first kiss. Ian brushed her cheek with his hand, and then she stood up and turned away. I watched as Alexia gathered up her things, leaving her backpack of treats behind. She tiptoed around sleeping bags and headed for the stairs. In another moment, she was gone.

When everyone woke up, they immediately noticed Alexia was missing, and Ian explained that she'd needed to leave. He didn't say any more, and he didn't need to. We were all exhausted. I could tell that the idea of leaving had occurred to most of us. People tried to distract themselves by playing cards, and eating whatever we had left. By noon, three more people gave up, and said their goodbyes. The rest of us slowly made our way through another day.

Outside, most of the parents had had enough. Our own parents didn't say anything, but they looked tired, and wet. They had seen enough to know, though, that we weren't leaving until we were ready, so there wasn't much point in telling us it was time. News reporters with interpreters interviewed Mario on the balcony several times. It was a bright spot, but still, no word. No change. Was there any point to all of this?

With Alexia gone, I spent most of my time reading. I'd come prepared. But it wasn't like anyone had energy to do much else. All around me the mood was quiet and subdued. Two days with no showers and minimal sleep will do that to people. We smelled. We were dirty. There was nothing pretty or romantic about the group of us still holding onto Veditz.

As it started to turn dark again outside, there was sound coming from downstairs, and I motioned to Ian that I heard something. He headed for the balcony. He stuck his head back inside, and asked Nya and Mario to join him. When they came back in, they called all of us around.

"Mr. Kennelly is coming up. We're letting him in. He says he needs to talk to us."

We gathered in a circle. Mr. Kennelly walked up the steps, and stopped in the doorway. He surveyed the room, and I tried to see us through his eyes. Disheveled, dejected, but still persistent. And now he was here to speak to us. Could it be good news?

He asked us to sit, and Mr. Kennelly found a spot on the floor next to Mario, his face serious. He put his hand on Mario's shoulder for a moment, and then started to sign.

"I want to tell you all how proud I am of you, and of all you've done here. The story has been on the news and you have a lot of people who understand why you're here. Mr. Giancola asked me to come talk with you, because he's heard from the governor's office."

There was a momentary rush of excitement, and everyone started signing at once: *"What's happening? Are they keeping school open? What did he say?"*

Mr. Kennelly's expression didn't change. He took a breath and began again.

"The Legislature has made the decision to keep Hawthorne open for one more year, so that you can all have time to find programs to go to after it closes. It will close the following year," he paused, as if he were choosing his signs very carefully, *"and they announced that the buildings and lands used for the Hawthorne School for the Deaf will be sold. It may become some kind of residence for senior citizens."* He took another breath, and there were tears in his eyes. *"I want you all to realize that without speaking out, the understanding to postpone the closure wouldn't have happened. You did that. You may not have changed what's going to happen to Hawthorne, but you have made a difference in how it happens."*

Everyone stared at Mr. Kennelly without moving, without making a sound. He was saying we had won something, but all that was clear was how much had been lost. But we were too tired to cry, or to fight, or to even say a thing. We all just sat there and stared.

"It's time to leave," he signed gently. *"You have given it everything you had to give. It's okay to go."*

When he stopped talking, everyone looked from Mr. Kennelly to Mario. Mario's face was flat, but he was running his hand through his hair. He looked at Ian and then Nya, and they seemed to silently come to a decision.

Mario nodded his head slowly, and looked at each one of us, his eyes scanning our uneven circle. If he wanted to say more, he didn't. Maybe he couldn't. He simply signed, *"Let's go."* And we all knew it was over.

It was so quiet, eerily quiet. No sound, no movement, as if there was nothing left to say or do. Then suddenly I heard a scream, and I realized it was Ciara. She screamed the word, "No!" It came out muffled and hoarse, but she screamed it at the top of her lungs, over and over, her hands fisted at her face. It was a painful scream, loaded with grief. I recognized it; I knew where it came from.

We all stared at her at first, stunned. Then Mr. Kennelly got up to go toward her, but Mario held up his hand, signaling him to stop. Mario went to her instead, opening his arms. She kept screaming, but when he reached her, she allowed him to wrap his arms around her, and hold her. I could still hear her, her head against his chest. In a few moments, she stopped.

I realized then that there was something special between them, a bond that went beyond the walls of Hawthorne, or any building. No matter what happened. Maybe they would stay in touch in the future, or maybe they wouldn't. Either way, they would be part of each other's lives forever. We all would.

Mario and Ciara sat down in a corner, as the rest of us slowly went into action. We gathered our things, trying to put Veditz back the way we'd found it. Deyquan handed me a trash bag and I picked up any stray wrappers and paper I could find. Everyone folded up their sleeping bags, and packed up their backpacks. We worked methodically, maybe because we were all exhausted, maybe to stay together for as long as possible.

I felt someone tap me on the shoulder, and turned to see Mario. *"Where is Ian?"* he asked, looking worried. I scanned the room. Mario signed *"disappeared."*

"Go find him," he said, and my mind went blank, thinking of where to start my search. Just as suddenly, an image popped into my head and I knew immediately where he was. I knew exactly where to find him.

I ran downstairs, slowing down as I reached the bottom. I turned the corner and stopped to lean against the doorway. There was Ian, sitting on the floor next the Wall of Pride with a book, a roll of tape and a pair of scissors. He'd turned on one light, the one focused on the pictures, but otherwise, the hall was dark. As I watched, he took the scissors and cut a small square out of the book. I squinted and saw that it was a yearbook. Ian took the picture he'd cut out and stuck it to the wall with tape. He wrote on a piece of paper and attached it underneath.

As I stared at him from the doorway, I thought of how I'd stood just this way so many times, sneaking up behind him, waiting to be caught. I could have done it again, but I wouldn't. Not anymore.

All those times, all I'd ever really wanted was to pull him closer. I no longer had to do that by playing games.

I walked towards him, stamping my foot on the floor to get his attention first. I didn't want to startle him. He glanced over at me as I approached. He looked so tired, and so sad. He motioned for me to sit next to him.

I knelt down on the floor beside him and looked at the yearbook. At a small school like Hawthorne, everyone gets to have their own page. Glossy pages full of photographs, writing and art. Ian was cutting out pictures of everyone.

"Can I do some?" I asked.

Ian handed me the scissors and the yearbook, and I continued cutting out pictures while he stuck them onto every available space on the wall, like a mosaic. When I handed him his own picture, the last one, he stared at it for a while before taping it on the wall. He stuck a blank piece of paper under it.

"What are you going to be when you grow up?" I asked him.

"I don't know," he answered, but he smiled as he signed it. *"We'll see."*

I looked up at the pieces of paper he'd posted under each of the yearbook photos. On each one he'd written the person's name, but otherwise they were blank.

A few minutes later everyone came downstairs. They stood around us and stared at what Ian had done. Nya and Ciara cried. Mario bent down and put his hands on Ciara's shoulders. Her face was dirty, and her hair knotted. She swayed slightly from side to side.

"You did it," he told her, *"you and I will be the last to leave."*

Ciara smiled, and Mario wiped her tears away. Then he asked her if she felt like walking or riding out, and when she chose riding, he had her climb onto his back. She rested her head on his shoulder.

"Everyone," Mr. Kennelly signed, *"everyone grab someone's hand."*

We grabbed hold of each other, making one long chain. I held onto Ian with one hand and Deyquan with the other. With Mr. Kennelly in front, and Mario and Ciara in back, we stepped outside.

15

I'd like to be able to say that following our poignant and heartfelt departure (that's what one reporter wrote) the Governor and Legislature suddenly realized the error of their ways and agreed to let Hawthorne stay open forever. They didn't. Things just don't work that way. They haven't changed their minds yet, and it's likely they never will. All anyone knows is that there's more fighting ahead, and as Ian said in the car on the way home, right before we both fell asleep, *"I'm not done."*

We got home at around two in the morning on Wednesday. After that, Ian and I slept for two days. We got up to eat a meal now and then, but mostly, we slept. Hawthorne closed for the rest of the week, and my parents had no choice but to let me skip a few more days of school. I was just too worn out. My bed never felt so good.

By the weekend we were stumbling around, and as we started to wake up, the spirit of the sit-in returned. Ian and I sat at the kitchen table and talked for hours. He wanted to know what I thought of everybody, and I wanted to know all the gossip he could come up with. Now, when he told his stories, I knew exactly who he was talking about. I knew Hawthorne in a way I'd never imagined knowing it, from the inside.

Monday came, with us back to doing what we always do: Ian on the bus to Hawthorne; me sprinting to school and sliding into my seat just before the bell. Or a few seconds late. This time, though, with a smile from Mr. Polin, a real smile that I didn't have to decipher because he quickly added, "Good job, Ms. Marks. You provided the perfect example of civil disobedience I needed for my lecture last week."

Then he winked and said, "And by the way, you're late. In case you were wondering."

Some things never change, and it's nice when they don't.

When I went outside for lunch I found Sandoval on the bleachers in our usual place. I hesitated before sitting down. He looked up at me and shielded his eyes from the sun with his hand.

"Hey," he said. He was squinting, and I couldn't tell if he was happy to see me.

"Hi."

"So, I hear you're some kind of...revolutionary," he said, breaking into a sly smile. "A revolutionary on a camping trip?"

I laughed, and sat down next to him on the stone steps. "I guess you could say that," I answered, looking out over the field, where a bunch of kids labored around the track. I leaned my elbows back on the step behind me.

"It must have been amazing," Sandoval said as he leaned back too. He sighed. A moment later, I felt his pinky link itself around mine. Suddenly I could feel my heart beating faster than is probably healthy. I waited for him to move, correct his mistake, run away, whatever. But he didn't. He didn't move. His pinky stayed there, wrapped around mine. No accident.

I remembered to breathe, and with that, my heart rate returned to some kind of normal. I took stock of what was happening. Sandoval was touching me. Sandoval and I were holding pinkies.

Nice things still happen.

Terrible things happen, and good things happen. They both, I'd come to realize, could happen to people I loved. They both could happen to me.

"It was pretty amazing." I nodded my head but I kept staring at the field, afraid to look at Sandoval. No, not afraid, the opposite of afraid. I was cherishing the feeling of his finger on mine, and I didn't want it to stop.

"I've never heard of anyone bringing chocolate bars to a sit-in," Sandoval remarked, and when I did look over at him, he was smirking. "That wasn't in any of the articles Mr. Polin made us read."

"They were our most popular item, thank you very much," I said, breaking into a grin.

Sandoval took his hand and laced his fingers through mine. A shiver fanned out across my whole body. Who knew holding hands could be so incredible?

"Whatever you say," he said softly. "You'd know best."

I nodded, looking into his crazy-beautiful eyes. "I do."

It was true. I know what I know.

And there's a whole lot I don't yet know, but I'm ready to find out.

Author's Note

This is a work of fiction. That said, when I first began the book ten years ago, I decided I wanted to do two things – find a way to incorporate my memories of a beloved friend, Lisa, and also share what I had observed in three years as secretary at the Massachusetts State Association of the Deaf in Boston.

When I first started writing, I used the name Lisa as I waited for another name for the character to come to me, but as time went on, I couldn't imagine her any other way. If you knew the real Lisa you may recognize her here, in the way her unique spirit infuses the fictional character. Did any of this actually happen? Of course. There were candy bars one birthday. We both had a crush on the same guy (twice). She often serenaded me. Most importantly, I can still remember how it felt to be in her company. Her friendship continues to be a very important part of me, and always will be.

Working at MSAD was a wonderful immersion into the Deaf community, and there are not enough words, or signs, to express my appreciation for Steve Nover and the many people who welcomed and supported me then, as well as later when I became a clinical social worker. Ian is the brother I never had, a completely made-up older sibling who I may continue to conjure up from time to time.

Waiting for a Sign would not be the book it is today without the help of many friends who generously offered me their time, suggestions and sensitive reads. So many people have shown me support and encouragement over the past ten years; only a few are included here. Thank you to Sherry Bergman, Rachel Cane, Steve Cariddi, Theresa Christensen, Janey Greenwald Czubek, Robert Danberg, Ria Davidis, Barbara Edwards, Matt Evangelista, Joanie Filler, Julia Fruchtman, Jennifer Groff, Nancy Hall, Kim Kelly Harriman, Lizzie Hirtenstein, Emily Rhoads Johnson, Livia Schachter Kahl, Li Hong, Samantha Liddick, Tamara Loomis, Jim Meyers, Patti Meyers, Laura Rosenfeld, Karen Shirley, Susan E. Ward and Juli Zeffert for their warmth and support in reading the book and providing helpful and important feedback. Special thanks go to Brennan Ruffing, whose insightful questions and encouragement were instrumental towards re-energizing me in pursuing the publication of this book.

A special thank you to Rose Leiman Goldemberg, of course. All there is to say is already in these pages.

Much thanks and deep appreciation go to my parents, Mordy and Zipora, and my sister, Leora. And finally, to Jon, Elie and Ari, who are everything that is sweet and funny and kind and sarcastic and lovely in my world – thank you.

CPSIA information can be obtained
at www.ICGtesting.com
Printed in the USA
LVOW12s2203300316

481459LV00004B/235/P